SHADOW BOY

SHADOW BOY

Susan E. Kirby

ORCHARD BOOKS New York

The author gratefully acknowledges the help and advice of

National Head Injury Foundation
333 Turnpike Road, Southborough Road, Massachusetts

Illinois Head Injury Association, Inc.
507 South Gilbert, LaGrange, Illinois

Ellen W. Miller, M.S., P.T.
Coordinator, Rehabilitation Program
Department of Physical Medicine and Rehabilitation
BroMenn Health Care, Bloomington, Illinois

A special thank-you to Julie Lynch, Ellen Lynch, and Linda Kirby for sharing personal experiences. Each has withstood life's trials with faithfulness, love, and courage.

Orchard Books, A division of Franklin Watts, Inc.
387 Park Avenue South, New York, NY 10016

Manufactured in the United States of America
Book design by Jean Krulis

10 9 8 7 6 5 4 3 2 1

The text of this book is set in 11 pt. Sabon.

Library of Congress Cataloging-in-Publication Data
Kirby, Susan E. Shadow boy / Susan E. Kirby. p. cm. Summary: After Artie suffers a closed-head wound in a car accident, adjustment and recovery are difficult for him, his sister, Cozy, and the whole family. ISBN 0-531-05869-7. ISBN 0-531-08469-8 (lib. bdg.) [1. Traffic accidents—Fiction. 2. Family life—Fiction.] I. Title. PZ7.K63353Sh 1991 [Fic]—dc20 90-7687

To Linda and Maury

with love

Prologue

He was lost in a vast emptiness.
Aware of darkness.
And rhythm.
Like water flowing past him.
Deep and hypnotic in its sameness.
He slept and slept.

He knew when the water changed.
It was the rhythm he noticed first.
It was louder, pulsing, throbbing.
Swelling over his head.
Yet it did not choke him.
He could breathe.
He could sleep.

The water was crashing against his head.
He peered through the murk.
He saw more water, endless water.
Cup hands. Kick. Flutter kick.

But he couldn't move the water.
He couldn't move in it.

Artie slept a restless, troubled sleep and awakened in cold terror.
The water was filling him.
Rushing in his eyes and his nose and his throat.
He kicked and thrashed his arms.

Sometimes he broke through to voices and figures that faded in and out.

In and out.
In and out, he floated.
Through endless time.
Until the darkness seemed more gray than black.
There were shadows beyond it.
And voices.
The voices made words he could not understand.
They would not leave him.
They touched and prodded him and spoke in a tone that said, "Swim harder."
Exhausted, he tried to retreat to the deep waters.
But they had receded, and he couldn't find them.

PART ONE

Chapter 1

The air was hazy. Artie was on a raft. A white raft on the lake in back of the farm. He was thirsty, uncomfortable, anxious. Voices whispered past his raft. Grandpa! Waving from the far shore. Calling to him.

He strained to hear, but the words were too faraway, and the water was rough. It was cold, too, and full of sound. It lapped up over the raft, chilling his skin. He shivered and peered at Grandpa off in the distance. But Grandpa had gone back to hoeing weeds from his garden. And Lady was with him, leaping. All four paws off the ground. Chasing a butterfly. Silly dog!

A bird came to his raft. A crow! A white crow, was it? Huge, with features like a human face, hovering just over the raft. It landed on his foot, pecking his bare toes. *Shoo!* He shook his foot. The crow dug in its claws. *Ouch!* Lady lifted her head and saw the bird. She barked and leaped into the lake. Grandpa hooked his thumbs in his overall straps. His face was wrinkled with laughter.

It's not funny, Grandpa! It hurts! The crow hurts. Grandpa answered. Artie strained to hear, but the words made no sense. The tone asked something of him. An asking tone. For what? *What, Grandpa? What?*

He was tired. He wanted to float away. His hand tightened on the raft pole. The soft warmth of it startled him, touching off prickles that ran down his arms and legs. He tried to let go, but the pole was stuck to his hand.

And the voice kept pestering him. Was it Grandpa? No, not Grandpa, it was his mother! He peered hard at the face. It came to him in three milky, wavy sections. He couldn't follow across and see it as a whole face. But the voice *was* his mother's voice. His mother had found his raft.

Exhausted, he closed his eyes.

A noise awakened him. He opened his eyes. It was all so blurred. The rope, the ball, the glove, the cap suspended over him, the dark window. Were there people watching behind the window?

He lay still, not making a sound. Someone came near him. A hand touched his, crawled up his arm, touched his chin. His skin prickled. The person spoke, but her words had no meaning. He gazed at the paper in her hand. Or was it a white flag? A flag ship? A ship flag?

There were voices. What were the words? He tried to hold his eyes open, but weariness settled around him. It was like a dark, thick cloud.

He slept.

Someone reached through the darkness and touched his hand. A voice reached him, too. A familiar voice. Through a hazy film, he saw his sister. It was Cozy!—she was holding his hand. He would tell her not to leave him. There were words in his head, words to tell her. But they spun like spokes on a wheel. They would not come together.

Cozy talked. Her words came too fast. His head was crowded with noise. There was space for only one voice, and that voice was the voice of his thoughts. His eyelids grew heavy. When he opened them again, Cozy was backing away. Growing dimmer. Disappearing.

Don't go! Don't go!

The words wouldn't come. He lifted his hand. It was heavy. He could only hold it a moment.

"Artie?"

His name! Cozy's face wavered cloudlike between him and the line from which hung the ball, the glove, and the cap. She said more words, words without meaning. He reached out and caught a part of her. It was her hair.

Her sharp cry brought strangers. Huge towering shapes in white. Fear rose in his throat. *Don't hurt me! Don't hurt me!* He'd run to the farm. To Grandpa. Grandpa and Lady, they'd help him.

The crowd of white bent over him, tied him down. They bound him to the cot. Then Cozy faded away.

Chapter 2

Therapy, they called it. Artie held the word in his mind. When there was motion, it was therapy. When there was pain, it was therapy. When there were asking voices, it was therapy.

"This is a tilt table," said a therapy voice. A woman's fingers were warm on his arm. They were red fingers. "Don't be afraid. You won't fall."

The words were separate blocks flowing into his ears. Building blocks. The first were solid. He could handle them with his mind. But the words kept coming. They piled together, layering, overlapping, colliding. He could not sort them out. A smoky gray filled his thinking space. His heartbeat quickened. *MomMomMomWhereareyou?*

"I'm going to crankthetableupright . . ."

There was movement beneath him. Slanting, slanting, upward! His stomach lurched. He gripped the sides of the table.

The therapy voice kept talking, but the words slid past him.

The table climbed like a seesaw. His head climbed; the

noise inside his head climbed, too. He clutched the table more tightly and closed his eyes. He saw pinpricks of light in the waves of darkness.

Still higher his head climbed. His heart pounded. Stop! Down! The words were there. He tried to blow them out. Like bubbles, the words grew and grew until they burst. But they burst without sound. He ground his teeth and stiffened his legs.

The table stopped. Artie opened his eyes. His head was higher than the woman's. But his feet were down where shoes belonged. Slowly, slowly his heart stopped pounding. His head stopped rushing. It was not so cloudy up here. The woman's red fingers patted his hand.

"All that lyinginbed . . .soeasytosleep . . . getyouuprightawhile."

He tilted his head to one side and stared back at her. He saw that her nails, not her fingers, were red. Her hair was dark. Her eyes were brown. He saw that there was another woman, too. With bright hair and specks across her nose. Specks. Specks called . . . specks.

The other woman came closer. She touched his hand and spoke to him.

She was quiet, waiting. He gazed back at her. She had a fluffy face. Soft like a pillow. She said more words, but he lost them.

She wanted something from him. But his hand was empty. He had nothing to give. She took his hand. He didn't like the rain. It was wet. He tugged free and wiped his hand on his leg.

"You hurtyourheadhere . . ." Her fingers left a shadow on his forehead, gray and worrisome. He reached up and brushed it away.

She nodded and said, "That's right, Artie." She said

other words, too, but his name stood apart from the rest of her words. On her mouth, it was a bright word, a red word. A song word.

"Iwanttohelpyou . . . sayhi . . . sayhi."

Her fingers touched his chin. They were warm and firm, pulling his jaw down. His lips parted.

"Hi . . . say . . . hihihi . . ."

She took his hand, and put it in front of her mouth. "Feel . . . H-h-h-hi . . . feel it?"

Slowly, slowly the darkness lifted. His heart beat fast, because he was looking at her, finally knowing what she wanted. It wasn't something in his hand. It was in his head. Rain trickled down, salt rain, and burned his eyes. He had what she wanted! The word was in there. *Hi*, he thought. He sent it along, out of his head.

But it didn't come out into the air where his ears could touch it. It was trapped inside him. Lost. He closed his mouth, opened it, tried again. Drew in his chest, pushed. He made a strangled sound, but not the word. The word was stuck, locked up inside him. No matter how he tried, he could not send it out.

Chapter 3

More therapy. And the tilt table. As the woman with the specks on her pillow face said, "This is a tilt table," he nodded and waved his hand. Up. Take him up.

It didn't make his stomach roll to go up, up, standing. There was no pain. It didn't make him dizzy to look down at his feet. He saw the cards in the woman's hand.

"Tell me, what is this picture?" said the woman.

There were lines and colors. One bright, blurry mashed-together picture. The bird was blue—it was blue.

"Bird. It's a bird," the woman said, and turned the card down.

Wait! Not fair! He shook his head and waved his hand.

"What is it, Artie? Do you want to see it again?"

He nodded. He wanted the mash picture. She held it up again. He pressed his lips together and formed a soundless *b*.

She pressed her lips together, too. Her eyes were eager. Go ahead, they said. "Bird." She said it for him again. "Try it, Artie. Bird."

Bird. Come down, you bird, you. Out. Out of my mouth. He pressed harder. Grunted in his throat.

"Keep trying. You can do it."

His lips turned in, one pushed against the other. His tongue touched them. But the sound would not come. Sweat was on his forehead. Ropes in his stomach twisted tight. He tried again. And again. Covered his eyes.

"Take it easy, Artie. Relax." The woman put her hands over his and pulled them away from his face. "That's it. Open your eyes. Come on now, don't be upset. Try again."

Try again. Try again. It was hard work. Hard, hard work. Something was wrong with his head. Not just the noise. One side was heavier than the other. He lifted his left shoulder, rolled his head toward it. And the noise shifted abruptly. It trickled off to the side. It was still there, but more distant.

He looked and could see her again. Bright hair, round face, speckled cheeks. He straightened his head and his vision blurred. He tilted again, and it worked!

It dumbfounded him that a trick so simple as tilting his head could make such a difference. The fog had lifted. The noise had softened. The blurry shapes had become clear. It was magic. Tilt was the magic.

"You're getting tired, aren't you? Hold your head up if you can, Artie." She touched his face, guiding his head away from his shoulder. "That's better, isn't it?"

Everything blurred! What had she done? He wrenched his face free and tilted his head. She took shape again. The bird picture, too. He pressed his lips together and thought, *Bird.* Thought it with anger. His whole head seemed to vibrate with the anger inside him.

But he could not say the word. Why couldn't he say that word?

Chapter 4

Something was cool on his tongue. Mmm. Thick on his throat. Like sweet paint. What was it called? Artie looked and looked for the word until his head whined and he had to stop looking.

"One more bite," said Cozy. The spoon came toward him, right through the thin curtain of fog. He couldn't touch the fog. When he tried, there was nothing there. The magic! Remembering, he tilted his head to one side, just as the spoon touched his lips. Something cold slid down his chin into his lap.

"Oops, sorry," said Cozy. "Sit still."

He could see her better now. Her yellow hair curled up over her ears. She had a scolding look on her face. No, not scolding. What was that look?

"Sit still." Her words echoed. He knew, then. They were in the rowboat, on the lake at Grandpa's. She was worried he'd turn the boat over. She was the oldest, but she couldn't swim as well as him. He tried to rock the boat just to tease her, but his hand touched a wheel.

It wasn't a boat after all. It was a chair. Puzzled, Artie

chewed his lip and tried to think what kind of chair it was. It had wheels on both sides. He looked for his mother, thinking she'd tell him. But she wasn't there.

"Dad took Mom home to rest," said Cozy. "He brought you some baseball cards. See? RyneSandbergMark-GraceandShawonDunston." She gave him the colored cards with strangers' faces on them. She said some more words, too, but they all ran together and got lost in that shadowy place in his head.

There was a feeling of fullness in his abdomen. A heaviness, and a twinge of pain. It triggered a dim message, here and then gone. He shifted his weight and turned toward the sound of a new voice. A merry, singalong voice. Cozy jumped up, taking the sweet paint with her.

"I'd about givenuponyou," she said to the girl.

"Sorry I'm late. Hi, Artie. Nicesweatsuit. Newisntit?"

The girl's arms were strong around him. Strands of yellow hair tickled his nose as a cold cheek brushed his. He smelled snow and sunshine all mixed together.

"Brrr! It's cold outthere. Wait'll youseeBiff. Hegotaperm."

The words came and came, too fast to keep up. Artie tilted his head and looked at Cozy. He saw her face change. He heard the words fly between them, but he didn't understand.

He stopped listening and stared at the other girl. She had bright colors like leaves. Scarf, coat, hat, hand-covers. She was shining and musical, like wind chimes. It made his head float to watch her. She had flowers in her hand. She smiled as she held them out to him.

Pink blurred in front of his eyes. Then the girl turned and the flowers turned with her. There was another voice, a boy's voice. Their words and laughter mixed together. Then the boy came over to him. He jammed his hands in his pockets and rocked back on his heels. "Hi, Artie," he said, and then more words. Lost words.

Artie squinted at the boy. He made out a square chin, a red nose and cheeks, downcast eyes, and fidgeting feet. Talking and rocking, talking and rocking.

The words slurred together like echoes from a deep well. Artie winced at the tightening in his belly. He reached for the fleeting message it brought. Reached and missed. He chewed the inside of his cheek. Noticed the boy waiting. For what? Artie lifted his hand out of his lap.

But the boy didn't want it. He backed away. Heaved himself onto the end of the bed. Swung his feet. Artie stared at the blurps his feet made. Gray blurps with short stubby laces. More talking and talking. The boy, the girl, and Cozy.

The boy laughed. He whistled through his teeth and gave the girl a push.

She laughed and pushed back. What were their words?

Artie bit his lips and gripped the arms of his bicycle chair as his abdomen cramped. The voices around him ran on and on, making a commotion in his head. He wanted to sift the sounds, take out the noise, hold on to the words. But he couldn't. Pain stabbed his lower stomach. He sucked in his breath, let it out, and pushed.

The boy stopped swinging his feet and looked at the girl.

She looked back at him. Punched his arm. He shook his head. She hit at him again.

Artie wrinkled his nose and breathed through his mouth. There was a warm, sticky dampness in his shorts. He pulled at the waistband of his sweatpants. Cozy came over to him.

"Wait, Artie," she said, and reached for the white box to push the black button.

Faces changed. The boy's, the girl's, Cozy's. Laughter

left the room. It was still. The whole room was full of quiet. He heard a distant bell. But no one answered the door. They just sat. Looking down, saying nothing.

The girl slipped off the bed and reached for her colors. The boy got up, too. The pink left Cozy's face. She lifted her chin and said words back to them. She followed the boy to the door.

But the girl came closer. She leaned down to him and kissed his cheek. Squeezed his hand. Said gentle words with his name mixed in.

The boy lifted his hand. Said Artie's name again.

Then it was only Cozy. She patted his shoulder. "It's okay," she said, and she kept patting his shoulder.

But her face looked broken.

Chapter 5

"December, January, February, March. Here's today. That's three months and one, two, three . . . days. Three months andfourdayssinceyouraccident."

From his bed, Artie watched Cozy turn the pages. Her words kept coming, but he stopped trying to catch them. The calendar game made him itch inside. All those days and days and days. He was not sure Cozy was telling him right. He tilted his head and looked at her closely.

"That's better. Pay attention."

Bossy! Just because she was biggest. It made Artie want to hit her. But he saw that she looked more tired than cross. And determined. He closed his eyes and sighed, trying to remember what it was she wanted him to do. The bicycle! That was it. If she'd just get off, and give him a chance. He could ride it without the training wheels. His hand curled around the cold bar. But when he opened his eyes, he saw it wasn't bicycle handlebars, but a rail. A bed rail. He looked around for his mother.

Watching him, Cozy said, "Mom went home for a while, remember? Dad and I cametokeepyoucompany."

His father lowered the newspaper he was reading. "Did you want something, Artie?"

Did he? Artie's hand tightened around the rail. He looked at Cozy. He pointed to the bicycle chair. Cozy got out of it. His father lowered the bed rail, then grasped Artie's hands and pulled him up until he was sitting on the edge of the bed.

Artie inched his legs over the side of the bed. His feet prickled as they touched the floor. His father pulled him out of the bed. The motion made Artie's head swirl. He sagged against his father. Cozy pushed the bicycle chair up behind him and buckled his knees. His father eased him down.

Artie closed his eyes, listening to the humming in his head, waiting for the dizziness to stop. When he opened his eyes again, Cozy was fastening a belt around his waist. His father was backing away.

"I think I'll go downstairs for some coffee," he said.

Artie wanted to go, too, but the sadness in his father's face confused him. What had he done? What had he done to make his father so sad?

"There you go," Cozy said. "Therapy's helping. You're getting stronger."

He knew her words. Even therapy, he knew that word. He knew that place. He thought of the tilt table as Cozy talked on. Her words came faster. It made his head hurt. He quit trying to keep up and let them pile up into one lost heap.

"Do you have to go to the bathroom?" She said it slowly. "The bathroom?"

Oh, that. He looked down at himself and searched for the pressure in his belly. Shook his head.

"Okay. But tell me if you do." She put a piece of paper

on the table and slid it in front of him. "Want to try again? Try to write?"

He looked at his hands. Left, right, right, left. He could not think which was which. She gave him a pencil.

"Write your name. Write 'Artie.' "

He ran his fingers along the edge of the paper. He held it up by two corners, then held it in front of his face. It was quiet behind the paper. The noise in his head gentled, too. He heard Cozy moving about.

"Artie?" she was saying.

He was well hidden. Away from her noise, her asking voice. If he kept quiet, maybe she would not find him there.

"You could at least try," she said.

He was careful not to move, not to give himself away. But his arms were growing tired, holding the paper. They tingled and ached, and slowly, slowly, drifted down. The paper, too.

Cozy was crouched in front of him, looking and looking. She touched his head where it left a shadow, and frowned. "I won't let you sit here and not try."

Her voice was low and full of hard crackly pieces. He opened his hand, but she did not take it. Instead, she wrapped his fingers around the pencil. It found a resting place between his fingers and thumb. A natural fit.

"Do it for me. Try real hard."

Artie looked down at the paper. Its whiteness, its silence. He let the pencil roll free, picked up the paper, put it in front of his face.

Cozy took it from him. She took the pencil, too, and moved it across the paper, leaving a skinny gray trail. A funny trail that crowded together, up, over, back, and around.

"Like this." She held the paper up for him to see.

He stared at the gray trail and saw it was not a trail at all. It was a word. His word! *Artie!* There was a pressure in his head, like a hand around a sponge. Squeeze, let go. Squeeze, let go. Artie, he thought. He opened his mouth and moved his lips: Artie, Artie.

Cozy's eyes widened. "Artie?" she said in a hushed voice.

He brought his head down. Moved his lips again. Made a sound in his throat. Pushed harder, more sound. Dropped his chin. "Arrr . . . rrr . . ."

"Artie," she said, her eyes large and shining.

He nodded. "Arrr . . . arrt."

"Artie, you talked!" Cozy laughed out loud. She flung her arms around him, squeezed him tight, and cried. "You talked! You finally talked!"

Chapter 6

Artie's mother kissed his cheek. "Work hard," she said. "I'll wait for you here." Then she waved to him from the doorway as the woman took him to therapy.

Remember, remember. It was in Artie's mind that he had to remember a thing so important as to tilt his head. The magic was in the tilt. When things blurred, tilt. When words ran together, tilt. When the noise was too loud, tilt. That was the magic.

He thought of it as the therapist helped him out of his bicycle chair. There was a bridge in front of him. He wanted to cross it and hear his feet pound against the rough boards. He wanted to run and run and run.

"Take hold of the rail first, Artie," said the therapy woman.

Rail? Rails were for trains. Inside his head, he heard laughter. But she was not laughing. She would not let go of his arm.

"Grab hold, Artie."

He could stand alone. But his head was heavy and unbalanced. It pulled him hard to the right. He grabbed one pole of the bridge.

The therapy woman was right behind him, holding his shirt. He lurched forward two steps. His legs were mushy! The nerves jumped beneath his skin.

"Very good, Artie. Left foot, lift it up. Follow with the right. You're getting stronger each day," said the therapy woman.

But he wasn't strong! Not his legs. They only worked half-right. "Half legs," he said.

"Is that how it feels? You lost some muscle tone after your accident. You have to work hard to get it back."

Accident? Was that why his legs were so heavy? Had he fallen? Yes, off his bicycle! Grandpa took off the training wheels. Dad was pushing, pushing, letting go. Faster and faster he pedaled, with Dad running behind him, Grandpa cheering. Faster. Wind in his face, in his eyes. Then the hole in the road, the front wheel dropping in and throwing him off, and he was skidding along the road. A hurting accident. That was it. Slowly, he tightened the muscle in his leg, lifted his foot, pushed it forward.

"Very nice, Artie. That's it."

He pressed down hard on the poles and tensed his arms. He gritted his teeth. He lifted the other foot. All that weight. He pushed his heavy, heavy foot forward.

"It's a good thing you're such a hard worker!" said the woman. "Your mom says the doors at home aren't wide enough for a wheelchair."

It was raining all over him. In his eyes. Burning. His legs were trembling with pain. His chest hurt. His breath squeezed in and squeezed out. He tilted his head. But there was no magic for his heavy legs.

"Keep working. You have to build up your muscles so you can get around on your own when you go home."

Therapy, he thought. Pain was therapy. Therapy was pain.

When he could make it no further, the woman helped him back to his bicycle chair.

His foot itched. He leaned forward and tried to scratch it. But the woman put her hand on his shoulder. She pulled him back and strapped him there, far away from his foot. "I'd better get you back. It's time to eat."

Eat? The passing door moved faster, in a blur. Eat? He forgot his itching foot. He tried to remember breakfast, couldn't. He tried to remember lunch, couldn't. His mother wasn't with him.

His head swam with the new thought. It was eating time, and she hadn't come. Where was his mother? Why hadn't she come? He swallowed the knocking in his throat and tried to think where she could be. He couldn't.

"She'll come later?" He said it like a question.

"Who?" the woman asked.

"Mom."

"Your mother's in your room, Artie. She's been here all morning."

She said it in a sure voice. Why was he so unsure? His face grew warm, for he knew by her sureness that she was right and he was wrong. His eyes were hot. His breath was uneven. What was wrong? Why was he unsure when everyone around him seemed so certain?

Chapter 7

Artie's mother hummed as she piled magazines, cards, letters, and pictures on top of the things she'd already put in the brown paper bag. There was something important happening. Something different from therapy. Different from the calendar game. March. March was the month in the calendar game now. And then what? Artie tried to remember. He was about to ask, when his father came in. Cozy was behind him, carrying Grandpa's suitcase.

She plopped the battered suitcase on the bed beside him. "It won't be long now," she said, grinning.

Until what? Were they going away? Artie ran his hand over the frayed lid of the suitcase. Grandpa's suitcase. Where was Grandpa? At home, gardening. Was March a gardening month? Peas, raw, right off the vine. He thought of Grandpa's big square hands pulling the string, peeling open the pod. With a dusty finger, he'd strip the peas free and toss them into his mouth, green and juicy and warm from the sun. A wave of homesickness passed over Artie.

"I want to go home," he said softly.

His mother kissed him briskly. "Tomorrow, Artie. Just

one more day. Be patient." She turned to Cozy and asked, "You remembered his socks, didn't you?"

Cozy opened the suitcase. She spilled out socks and shoes and a sweat suit that looked big enough to fit Artie's father. "It's the Chicago Bears, see?" She held up the navy-and-orange sweatshirt. "Dad and I picked it out for you. What do you think?"

"It's too big," he said.

"I tried it on myself," said his father. "It'll fit you just fine."

Although his father did not smile, Artie was certain he was teasing. Just like when he put on Dad's old army boots and marched around, and his father laughed and said, "Hey, boots! Where are you taking that boy?"

"We weren't sure about the shoes. Want to try them on?" Cozy asked.

They were clean and new. Not a scratch. There were no strings. Just straps. And they, too, looked big enough to fit his father. Feeling tired and confused, he pushed the shoes away.

Cozy's face fell. "I told you he wouldn't like them," she murmured.

His father simply shrugged. He left and came back with popcorn and soft drinks. Artie's was orange-flavored. He sucked it down greedily, even though his mother kept patting his hand, saying, "Slow down—you're going to choke."

Orange was Grandpa's favorite, too. Where was Grandpa? Why wasn't he here? Was it one of those things he should know? Or was it a secret they were keeping from him?

There was a dark, shadowy cloud in his mind. Partly hidden by that cloud was a carefree, laughing boy. A boy who knew the answer to most of the things that seemed to elude Artie. There was something familiar about that boy. But when Artie closed his eyes, trying hard to see him clearly, the boy faded until there was nothing left but a nagging uncertainty.

Chapter 8

Artie recognized it. His father's car! His father was in the front seat, waiting. There was only one seat left. Cozy would want it—she would want the front. Artie swung around in his bicycle chair and looked at her. "I get the front seat!"

To his surprise, Cozy laughed and said, "Okay."

His mother laughed, too. She unlatched the door and called across the seat to his father, "Did you hear that, Walt? Artie wants the front seat."

"What else is new?" said his father, and everyone laughed again. Like lighthearted music.

'Watch your head," said his mother, as he got out of the bicycle chair. She held onto his arm while he eased himself into the car. He picked up his legs, swung them in.

"All set?"

He nodded. His mother leaned in. She strapped the seat belt across him and pulled it snug, then climbed into the backseat. He turned and looked around at Cozy. He wanted to say, "It's my turn for the front seat!"

She smiled and said, "We're going home."

Home! It was a word in his mind, but no picture. It was a feeling, too. His heart beat fast: boom-boom, home-home. His father turned the key, and the car pulled out of the shade and into the sunlight.

So bright! Pouring light on his face. He squinted and batted watering eyes. The car turned onto the street. On both sides, there were cars. In front of them, too. All colors, bright and dull. Swishing, braking, turning. He flattened himself against the seat, caught his breath. So much moving, so fast! There was sound, too. Cars humming, purring, coughing, honking. A truck with a bucket that creaked and clanged. A bus with a deep roar surging past, trailing smoke.

"Hold still!" he said, feeling small and frightened.

On they went, under a highway, over a bridge. Past tall buildings with glaring windows. Sidewalks and people and lights that changed colors. Too much, too, too much. It stunned him, the motion, the color, the noise rushing past.

He closed his eyes and rubbed them hard, watching the skinny lines and circles shift. But only for a moment. They were moving fast. He would miss . . . He didn't want to miss . . . something . . . something. He was waiting.

Dimly he heard his mother say, "Here's our building, Artie."

His heart pounded. His ears roared. Slow, slower went the car, until it had stopped. He gazed at the building. Faded red bricks. Wide steps. Windows and windows, climbing higher. He knew then, what he was searching for.

Where was the grass? The big old tree, the rope and the tire? Where was the clothesline? The black pump? The leaning barn and the pond? Bewildered, he turned and looked back at his mother. "Where's Lady?"

Her shining eyes dimmed; her mouth drew down. "Artie, Lady was Grandpa's dog."

Yes! Grandpa's dog. Chasing chickens. Diving into the lake after him, her sleek head cutting the water, her nose in the air. He held tightly to the vision and asked, "Is she here?"

"Honey, Lady's been gone a long time. Grandpa, too. We live here now, on the second floor. Remember?"

Heat crept up his neck and flooded his face. He knew she wouldn't say it if it weren't true. He looked at the building again. Looked and looked while his mother helped him out of the car.

He started up the steps, Mom holding one arm, Dad holding the other arm, Cozy running ahead to open the door. He knew, just as she opened it, that the walls would be white, the carpet red. He walked in, knowing each thing when he saw it. Knowing the mailboxes. The elevator. The needle above it. With the knowing came a sick, wrenching feeling, a feeling of grief and loss.

This was his home, not the house in the country. Lady was dead. And Grandpa was dead, too. He clutched his mother's hand and looked in his head for the missing piece—the chunk between Grandpa's house and this. Tears filled his throat, but when he opened his mouth, it was laughter that came.

His mother's arms closed around him. "It's okay, Artie. You're tired, that's all. Everything's going to be all right."

PART TWO

Chapter 9

Cozy pointed out the banner that stretched across their living room wall. She said, as Artie gazed at it, "The kids from school sent it. There must be hundreds of signatures. See what Biff wrote? 'Hang tough, dude.' Sounds just like him, doesn't it? Kurt Parks drew the skull-and-crossbones. Nobody asked for his two cents' worth, but you know how he is. And look down here. Star drew the flowers. Pretty good, isn't it?"

Did he understand? Did he recognize the names? Biff, his best friend; Star, her best friend; Kurt Parks, nobody's friend. His vacant expression gave no clue about what he did or didn't know. He looked thin and weary and lost. And yet this was the best he had looked since the day after Thanksgiving, when he'd jumped his skateboard off a curb into the path of an oncoming car.

"Sit down here on the sofa, Artie. Or would you rather go to your room?" asked Cozy's mother.

Artie looked confused by the question. Her father said, "Cozy made a cake. Do you want some cake?"

Artie shook his head.

"Would you like to lie down for a while?" asked her mother.

Artie nodded and let his parents ease him down on the sofa. Cozy's mother took off his shoes and put a cushion under his head. He was asleep almost instantly.

"He's so frail." Her mother touched the smudged hollow beneath one eye.

Cozy saw the sadness in her father's eyes as he turned sharply away. She went quietly to the kitchen and got her lopsided cake from the refrigerator. The icing was too thin. Her lettering, *Welcome Home, Artie*, had run together. Her eyes filled with tears. She reached into the pantry for a napkin, and the balloons that she had so happily blown up and stashed there spilled out and drifted to the floor. Hearing footsteps approaching, she wiped her eyes and wadded the napkin into her pocket.

Her father came in, silently making a path through the balloons. Her mother followed a moment later. She picked up a balloon and smiled.

"That was a nice idea, Coze. Artie loved balloons when he was little. Remember, Walt?"

Her father gave a silent nod and went on making coffee. Cozy poured herself a glass of milk.

"I could eat a piece of that cake," said her father.

Her mother opened her mouth as if to object, then nodded instead. They sat at the table, surrounded by scattered balloons, eating cake and saying very little.

It wasn't much of a party.

Chapter 10

Artie stood motionless, watching the dog. He had followed it to the empty lot, trying to think what it was called. Not its name. He didn't think he knew the dog. But its breed. That he should know.

Stupid lost word. Stupid freakin' lost word.

Thinking he might ask Cozy, he looked around and realized he was alone. He didn't mind. It would give him time to think whether he should ask her or not. Some things he could ask and she would answer in a way that made it all right to have asked.

"Hi, dog. Hi, there, you good dog, you." He stroked the dog's soft ears. The tags on the dog's collar jingled as he wagged his tail and sniffed Artie's hand.

He was not a large dog like Lady had been. Not a collie dog. This dog's brown velvety ears drooped like the tongues on a pair of Hush Puppies. His body was black with white patches. His legs were white with spots, irregular paint-splatter-looking spots of faded red and blue-black.

Tick, he thought. Red-and-blue tick. And for a moment,

he was elated. He grinned and said, "Tick." But in the open air, it didn't sound right. Tick had to do with clocks. Tick-tock, tick-tock. What did tick have to do with dogs? He couldn't get it right in his head.

What was the dog called? Stupid word. Stupid freakin' word.

The dog moved away, nose to the ground, making snuffling sounds deep in his throat. He parted the grass with his nose, sniffed again, and then rolled over. Artie watched as the dog came to his feet, shook himself off, and trotted away. The word still had not come. He shoved his hands into his pockets, his shoulders sagging.

"Artie?"

Cozy! She would know. He turned to ask, but her eyes were wild, and it confused him, made him forget his question. She was gasping for breath, and sweating.

"Artie, you scared me!" she panted.

Artie looked down, checking himself over. He was wearing a blue sweatshirt with the word *Nike* printed across it. His pants were zipped. And his shoes—the thick velcro straps didn't seem right on his feet, but they weren't frightening. "How?" he asked finally. "How did I scare you? Did you think I was someone else?"

"No, I didn't think you were someone else—I thought you were lost. I've been looking all over for you."

"I wasn't lost. I was here."

"Where is 'here'?" she asked.

Artie looked across the grassy lot. Did it have a name, like the dog? His heartbeat quickened. He looked at the screen in his head, the one his mother told him was there, where familiar things were kept. He saw in fast forward a whole instantaneous reel of places, jumbled, overlapping, scrolling like the monitor on his father's computer. If the grassy lot was there, he couldn't separate it from the other places. But he didn't want to tell her that, for he suspected it was a thing he should know. So he waved his hand and said, "Right here."

Her voice became gentle. "Never mind, it doesn't matter. Let's find Star and go home. Mom'll be worried."

That puzzled him, too. He took a chance and asked, "Why would she worry?"

"Because we're late. Whenever we're late, she worries. Understand?"

Not really. But Cozy was ahead of him now, waiting for him to catch up, and he didn't think he should ask.

Chapter 11

"You *lost* him? How could you lose him?"

For three days, Cozy had put off telling her mother. "Star and I were talking, and I guess, for a minute, I kind of lost track of him."

"But I depend on you!"

"He hadn't gone far."

"How far?"

"Just the empty lot where we used to play."

"Lost!" cried her mother, realizing what could have happened.

Cozy blinked back tears. "I'm sorry, Mom. It scared me, too."

"He must have been terrified."

She thought it over for a moment and then shook her head. "I don't think so. He didn't act scared. That's something."

"What? That he doesn't know enough to be scared when he's lost?"

Cozy ducked her head. Her mother's voice collapsed into a sigh. She put down the potato peeler and patted her shoulder.

"I'm sorry, Coze. It's just that we can't be careless. He's so vulnerable."

Cozy nodded. *Right here*, he'd said with a wave of his hand. He hadn't said it was the lot where he and his friends used to spend so much of their time playing football and kickball, baseball and soccer. But that didn't mean . . .

Cozy watched her mother cut a potato. She helped herself to a raw wedge and talked around it. "You don't think it's significant, then? That he found his way to the lot?"

Her mother's hands stopped. "You mean, maybe he *did* know where he was? Just not in a way he could verbalize?"

"Right. Maybe a sort of sixth sense led him there."

"Could be, I guess." Cozy's mother resumed peeling potatoes, frowning slightly.

Discouraged, Cozy sighed. In the month and a half since Artie had come home, his rapid strides had slowed down to plodding, small gains. Although his vision was almost fully recovered, his motor skills were poor. His attention span was short. He couldn't read very well, or find his way around what used to be familiar territory.

Time, time, and more time—that's what his doctor said a head injury required. Two years, five years, maybe ten, of ongoing recovery.

Cozy crossed to the window, thinking back to the day of Artie's accident. A movement in the alley below caught her eye. It was a buff-colored stray cat picking its way through an overflowing garbage bin. Through the open window came the sound of a freight train rumbling past the back doors of Chippewah Industry. The cat leaped free of the dumpster. Cozy thought it was the noise of the train that had frightened it—until she spotted Kurt Parks dashing up the alley, throwing pebbles. She pushed her nose against the screen. "Kurt, you jerk! Cut it out!"

Kurt tipped back his head, grinning up at her. "I wasn't trying to hit him."

"Yeah, I'll bet." She snapped the window shut, and moved to the end of the counter to pick through the mail. There was an Express Mail envelope at the bottom of the stack. She waved it at her mother.

"A sale?"

"Maybe. It's a historical piece I wrote a year or so ago. *Yesteryear* kept it on file."

"And now they want it?"

"If I can revise it," her mother said.

"How much?"

"Three-fifty."

"Three hundred and fifty or three dollars and fifty cents?"

"Your confidence is overwhelming."

Cozy grinned. "That's great! Aren't you excited?"

Her mother nodded, but said doubtfully, "It's a short deadline, though, and it needs more research."

"But you *like* research."

"It takes time, though, the revising. And then there's Artie."

"I'll stay home and help with Artie."

"That's sweet of you, Coze, but you have to go to school. I'll try to manage it."

As Cozy took the plates from the cupboard, her mother added, "That's Artie's job. Leave them on the counter for him."

"He's watching *Oprah*."

"But he needs to do the jobs he *can* do. And he needs to get away from that television." Her mother rinsed her hands and went out to get him.

Chapter 12

Credits were flashing on the TV. They moved too fast; Artie could not read them.

"It's time to set the table, Artie. The show's over, anyway," his mother said, starting toward the knob.

"No, wait! I can get it." Eagerly, Artie fumbled for the remote control. When he found the button labeled *Power*, a surge of satisfaction went through him. He held it up, showing her. "See?"

"That's good, Artie." Her smile calmed the anxious spot inside him. He smiled, too.

"Show me how you turn it off," she said.

A splash of color on the screen caught his attention. "Just a minute."

"Please do it now, Artie. I need your help in the kitchen."

"I like this. Just a minute!"

On the television screen was a colorful cartoon picture of Oprah Winfrey. She was dragging letters around. HARPO. HARPO. A clown word, a word that didn't fit? No! OPRAH backwards! It fell into his mind just like that. He sucked in his breath, amazed. Yes, that's what it was.

HARPO, OPRAH. Did his mother see it, too? He waited for her to comment, and when she didn't, he hesitated, beginning to doubt his own discovery.

"Oprah," he said. "Did you see that?"

"Turn it off now. It's time to set the table."

So it wasn't anything to mention. Somehow, he had thought it was. It had seemed like a startling revelation. His elation evaporated. He was lost. What mattered? What didn't? He couldn't distinguish. His head was full of deep shadows and information hidden in a thick fog. He knew it hadn't always been that way.

"It's a real help to me when you set the table," his mother was saying.

Warily, he followed her into the kitchen. He looked at the table, then the chairs, and wasn't sure where to start. He glanced at Cozy. She might help. Not wanting to ask her, he complained, "I have to set the table."

But Cozy just pointed out the stack of plates. Once more he looked at the table, the four chairs. His stomach tightened. It was a puzzle. Every piece had its own place, and it was important to put each of them where it belonged.

He picked up a plate. It was white with a narrow blue band around the edge. Turning it over in his hand, he asked, "Is it Dad's?"

"What do you think, Artie?" said his mother.

"I was asking Cozy."

His mother smiled and patted his arm. "I know, dear. But think about it yourself. The plates are all alike, aren't they?"

He spread them out in a line. "Except for this one," he said, pointing to one with a discolored spot.

"Then does it matter which one goes where?"

It was a test. There was only one right answer. His heart

beat loudly in his ear—bleep-bleep, bleep-bleep, don't-know, don't-know. He twisted his mouth to one side, scratched his lip, and shuffled his feet. "I don't know."

The phone rang. Cozy's mother reached for it, saying, "Help him think, will you, Cozy?" as she moved away.

"They aren't monogrammed, Artie," Cozy said.

He didn't know the word. Why wouldn't she help him? Was she angry? Was it something he'd said, or done? Miserably he stared at the plate, turning it over and over. "Is it Dad's? Is it, Cozy?" he asked again, when he could stand it no longer.

Cozy glanced at their mother, who was still on the phone, and nodded. A wave of relief went over him. She wasn't mad after all. And he'd gotten one right. He knew where his father sat. He sat with his back to the stove. Circling the table, Artie put the plate down, then went back for a second plate. "Is it Mom's?"

"It doesn't matter, Artie. Plates aren't like toothbrushes. Anyone can use any plate. Do you understand?"

"Yeah, I know," he said quickly, though he hadn't known. He passed out the plates one at a time. But was that all? The table with the four plates didn't look right. Faces without ears. What else? What else? He glanced at Cozy but couldn't bring himself to ask her again. So he searched the space in his head, the one his mother called a screen, and he saw the table as it had been a long time ago, when he was that other boy. Forks. Forks! Quickly, he crossed to the refrigerator. Cool air and the smell of leftover chili hit him in the face.

"What are you looking for?" Cozy asked.

"Forks."

"You won't find them in there."

Another mistake! His face grew hot.

His mother put her hand over the mouthpiece. "Forks don't have to be kept cold, do they, dear?"

Cold? Cold forks? He couldn't think. He could scarcely hear above all the confusion in his head.

"Try the drawer," Cozy suggested. She pulled it open.

And there they lay, all stacked in one slot. His head grew quiet, and the jittering in his stomach relaxed. He picked up a fork, placed it beside his father's plate, returned for another, and for another, until all the forks were in place. He did the knives next, and then the spoons.

At last the table looked right. But he felt no pleasure in it. It was a baby job, and he hadn't been able to do it right. Not without questions.

Chapter 13

"Coze, did you order a pizza?"

"No, why?"

"There's a fellow out here from Speedy Pizza. He's got a pizza and he's asking for you."

Cozy slammed her Business Ec. book shut and rolled off her bed. "What kind of pizza?"

"If you didn't order it—"

"I didn't. But as long as it's here, it wouldn't hurt to ask." Cozy squeezed past her mother. At the end of the hallway, she stopped short. Micah Daniels! He was a transfer student she'd only met for the first time two weeks earlier in English class. She was turning back, intending to rake a comb through her curls and change her battered slippers for shoes, when he looked past her father and spotted her. His ears turned red, but his smile was cocky.

"Hi. I brought you a pizza."

"Great! What kind?"

"The complimentary kind. It's Speedy Pizza's promotional campaign. Every day, we pick one name out of the city directory for a free pizza. This is the first time it's been someone I know."

Cozy caught the look that passed between her parents. So did Micah. He grinned, adding, "Figure the odds on that one, huh?"

Her parents smiled and discreetly moved into the living room. But Artie got up from the sofa and came to join Cozy at the door asking, "Is it for us?"

Cozy nodded and put a hand on his arm. "This is my brother, Artie. Artie, this is Micah Daniels."

Artie blinked, still studying the box. "Are we going to eat?"

"You'd better, before it gets cold. We've got our reputation to uphold." Micah pointed to his cap, which was emblazoned with Speedy Pizza's motto, *Pipin' Hot on Delivery.*

Artie pulled at his lip and frowned. "Do I have to set the table?"

"It isn't dinner—you don't have to," Cozy said quickly.

"Artie, come with me and we'll get some napkins. You'll stay and have some, too, won't you, Micah?" Cozy's mother intervened.

"I can't. I've got more deliveries," Micah said, giving Cozy the pizza.

Cozy passed it on to her mother, who said, "At least let us give you something for your trouble."

Cozy's father took out his billfold. But Micah backed out the door, insisting, "Not on a complimentary pizza. It's a rule."

"Say, this kid's all right!" said her father.

Ignoring Cozy's embarrassment, her mother smiled at Micah and said, "Cozy, why don't you walk him down?"

"Yeah, walk me down," Micah agreed.

As the door closed behind them, Cozy asked, "Where did it really come from?"

"The pizza? The address was next door's. But the lady wouldn't accept it. She claimed she hadn't ordered it, and she doesn't even like pizza."

"Some kid probably called it in as a joke," Cozy said. "I'll bet it was Kurt Parks. That's the kind of thing he does."

"It could be," Micah agreed. "Though if that's the case, the joke was probably on me as much as your neighbor. I doubt it was a coincidence that Speedy Pizza got the order."

"You know Kurt, then?"

He grinned. "Doesn't everybody?"

"And you're not mad?"

"Why should I be? I get paid by the hour." He grinned again as they walked onto the elevator, and added, "And I ran into you. Nice bonus."

Caught off guard by his frankness, Cozy ducked her head. Her big toe was poking through the hole in her seedy slippers. Retracting it, she said, "We could save the pizza, if you want to stop back later."

"It'll be too late. Besides, they take my pizza wheels away from me when I clock out."

"Your pizza wheels?"

"Yeah. They're parked out in front. I'll show you."

She followed him into the twilight, and he pointed out a battered orange hatchback. "A fine piece of machinery. It shakes off the toppings if I climb over thirty-five."

Cozy laughed and followed him to the curb.

"I heard about your brother's accident," he said as he climbed in the car. "How's he doing?"

Not sure whether he was asking out of politeness or whether he was really interested, she said cautiously, "Pretty good. It's going to take some time, though. And lots more therapy."

"Well, you've got him. That's the important thing."

She nodded and thanked him again for the pizza. He waved as he drove away, and called, "See you in English." But it was his words about Artie that she took back upstairs.

Chapter 14

Artie was looking for his jacket when he found his high-tops. Good old shoes! How long had they been lost?

He sat on the floor and held them in his lap. He examined the broken stitches, the blue soles, the white leather, scuffed bare on the toes, the tiny pinprick air holes. Good old shoes. *His* shoes. He plucked at the soiled laces.

"Did you find your jacket?" asked his mother.

Artie lifted his head. "Look, Mom. Look what I found—my old shoes."

His mother joined him at the closet door. "So you did. Let's have a look."

He stood and gave her one shoe, holding on to the other. It whispered as she turned it in her hand. "There's sand in them," she said. "You wore them on the beach, remember?"

The beach? It wasn't the picture in his mind. He shook his head. "No, playing basketball," he said. "These are my basketball shoes."

His mother's mouth opened in surprise; then she smiled. "We *did* buy these for basketball. Your first year. Remember, Artie? You knew exactly what shoes you wanted. But we had a hard time finding them. We shopped and shopped, until finally I told you to choose something else. But Dad said we'd look a little longer, and he hung in there until we found them at a sporting goods store in Evanston."

There were no pictures of that shopping trip in his mind. But Artie liked the story. "Tell me again," he said, and when she did, he stroked his shoe and thought out loud, "Dad's nice, isn't he?"

"Yes, he's a good dad," she said.

Artie pulled at one velcro strap, then the other. His mother said, "Artie, your old shoes won't fit. You outgrew them a long time ago."

"They'll fit," Artie said. "Yes, they will, Mom. They're good old shoes."

"But your feet have grown."

"They'll fit," Artie said again. He kicked off the shoes that belonged to someone else and straightened his sock. "See?" he said, slipping his toes in. But his heel would not go down. He tugged and tugged, but he could not force it down. *They belonged to that other boy. The shadow boy.*

"See what I told you, Artie? You've gotten tall, and your feet are too long," his mother said.

"Long tall feet," he echoed, and though he was sad that his foot wouldn't fit into the shoe, he liked the words. He laughed. "Long tall feet—that's funny."

His mother grinned. "Long tall shoes from Timbuktu, Tennessee."

He laughed again. "Good clown words, Mom."

"You and your clown words," she said, smiling, as she gave him back his shoe. "But what about your jacket?"

Wishing things didn't need finding, Artie complained, "I don't like looking."

"I know. But you make some interesting discoveries when you search for things. Like your old shoes, right?"

He thought about that and nodded.

"Why don't you look some more?"

"But they aren't lost," Artie said, clutching both shoes in his arms.

"I meant your jacket. Jackets are kept in the closet, and you're getting very close."

He didn't want to think about it or look for it. Jutting out his chin, Artie said, "I don't care. I don't want it!"

She shrugged and sighed. "If you don't find it soon, we can't walk to the post office."

"I don't care," he said again.

"All right, then. You may as well get started early and set the table for dinner."

"Freakin' table."

"Artie, I don't like that word very much."

"It's a clown word," he claimed, and his mouth wiggled, because he knew that it wasn't.

She leaned her head to one side. "You wouldn't be teasing me, would you, Artie?"

He nodded, saying, "I like to tease."

"And you like going for walks, too, don't you? But if we don't go right away, it'll be time to start dinner and we won't be able to go at all."

"Can't I go by myself?"

"One of these days, you will." She gave him a hug, and smiled. But her smile was shaky, and it made him wonder why he *couldn't* go by himself. He felt certain that other boy had.

Chapter 15

It was a long walk. But the sun was shining, and the air smelled fresh and clean. They walked past green lawns with flowers and bushes and tall trees with heavy branches. Then there were buildings and concrete. His mother pointed out the street signs. He listened to the names. Although they sounded familiar, they did not stay in his head.

"Can you show me the way?" asked his mother.

"Where?" he asked. He had forgotten where they were going.

"To the post office."

He stopped and looked around. What lay behind him was familiar, but what lay ahead was a question mark. His heart beat faster. His eyes felt as if they were right on the edge between knowing and not knowing. He would see Penny's Beauty Shop with the big penny painted on the window, and his eyes would know it. There! There! they would shout to the space in his head. They would pass the used bookstore that looked as dusty as the old books in the window. Yes! Yes! his eyes would say. Then the pet store. Right! The pet store! He pressed his face to the glass.

A little white puppy with sad eyes stared back at him from behind the bars of his cage.

"If I had a penny, I'd buy that puppy and let him go."

"I don't think a penny would be quite enough, Artie. Besides, he'd get hurt, wandering free."

"Maybe not," Artie said. "Anyway, I'd let him go."

His mother opened her mouth to disagree, then closed it again and just smiled. But he knew that inside she was disagreeing, so he said again, "I would, Mom. I'd let him go."

They mailed his mother's letters and were starting home when he heard the train whistle. He turned and looked back, but he couldn't see the train. "Is it our train?"

"Our tracks, you mean?" His mother nodded. "They run along behind the box factory and straight east, just a block behind our building."

"Let's go see."

"Artie, it's a dingy little back street, not a good place to walk."

"I want to see the train. I like trains."

He could see in her face that his mother didn't care about trains. But she went anyway. And it was just like the stores they passed. When they came to the factory and the railroad tracks, his eyes said, Yes! to the space in his head. His heartbeat quickened and he grinned. "They make boxes here. Don't they, Mom? Don't they!"

"Yes, they do. Crates and pallets, too. They load them onto the boxcars and take them all over the country. Your class came on a field trip here once. Remember?"

He looked for that picture in his head, but it wasn't there. He didn't tell her, though. He just kept walking until he could see the train cars. A few were on the side track, standing still. But off in the distance, he could see a long line of boxcars moving down the tracks.

He watched until the train was out of sight, and his mother watched with him.

"We've got to go now," she said. As they walked, she pointed out street signs and said the names for him.

They did not stop again until they came to a trampled lot where children were playing. It was the ball that caught Artie's attention, patched and scuffed and dirty with age. Suddenly there scrolled in his mind a picture of just such a ball. A picture of him and Biff playing kickball in this lot. Cozy and Star were there, too, way out where the weeds were tall.

"Do you know this place, Artie?" his mother asked.

He nodded; he did know it. Baseball, kickball, cops and robbers. A lemonade stand. But where was Biff? There was a faint humming in his head as he looked around. He and Biff had been good friends. Where *was* Biff? He began to sweat, wanting to ask, but not wanting to ask. Biff was in his head, in the old scenes that were unfolding. A wave of longing, loneliness, and fear made him shiver.

"Did you want to watch the children awhile?" his mother asked, and he nodded. He did not want to leave this place until he remembered. Remembered about Biff.

The noise and distraction of the children playing kickball made it hard for Artie to think. His head hummed louder as he watched them slide in the grass and listened to their yelling. One girl kicked the ball clear to the sidewalk. It rolled to a stop at Artie's feet.

"Home run!" she cried, strutting around the bases, her braids slapping her back.

A red-faced boy trudged after the ball. Artie picked it up and turned it over in his hands. Wiping his forehead with his grimy sleeve, the boy grumbled, "It's not fair. She won't play unless we make the sidewalk an automatic home run."

Artie's mother smiled and motioned for Artie to give the boy the ball. But Artie held on to it a moment longer. Biff had a ball just like it, scuffed and scratched, low on air. Artie turned the ball in his hands and felt the weight of it before giving it to the boy.

As they walked on, Artie drew a deep breath and finally asked his mother, "Was Biff in the accident, too?"

"In your accident? No, honey. Biff was there, but he didn't get hurt."

"Did he move away?"

The look on his mother's face reminded him of curtains at the kitchen window. She was pulling them closed—walking briskly. "No, Artie, he didn't move away. He came to see you at the hospital once."

"I don't remember."

"I didn't think you would."

Artie scratched his ear. "I don't see him anymore."

"I think Biff intends to come see you, but he just doesn't find the time."

Her answer rang loudly in his mind. The scenes with Biff were fresh in his head. They used to have so much time to spend together, laughing and shouting and running and riding. He looked at his mother, at the wrinkles around her mouth and the anxious flicker in her eyes. He wanted to ask her why Biff didn't come by the house anymore, and why he didn't go to Biff's house. But the noise had grown too loud in his head. Still, it made him sad, thinking about Biff.

"Do you remember when you and Biff thought you'd collect lightning bugs for a chemical company?" His mother tipped her head to one side and hooked her arm through his. The wrinkles around her mouth relaxed. "You couldn't have been more than eight or nine. You boys begged us to take you to the park at dusk. Then you brought your jar of bugs home and put them in the refrigerator overnight."

It was not in his mind, that picture.

His mother laughed. "You wanted to count them. You both thought they were dead, so you poured them out on the kitchen table."

"Were they dead? Were they?"

"No. The refrigerator had chilled them enough to make them lie still. When they'd been on the table a minute or two, they warmed up. By the time I realized what you two were up to, there were lightning bugs all over my kitchen!"

Artie laughed, too. It was a clown picture—lightning bugs in his mother's kitchen.

"Biff held the jar while you raced around trying to catch them. Bugs everywhere! Was I mad!" She wiped her eyes.

"But now you're laughing," he said, puzzled why what was not funny then was funny now.

"It's a memory, Artie. Memories often make us smile." Suddenly she became serious. She paused at the curb and looked up at him. "But memories are in the past. They're like lightning bugs and friends. Sometimes you have to let them go."

"You have to let friends go, too?" Artie asked, thinking not only of Biff, but of the other boy. The boy who seemed so close sometimes. Yet so elusive.

Chapter 16

Artie stood at the kitchen window with the curtain bunched in his hand. The breeze stirred his hair. He looked down at the alley, watching a cat.

It was a yellow cat, long and lean with tattered ears, crouched low near the end of the alley. For some time, it moved nothing but its tail. Then all at once it leaped to one side and away. Seconds later, a boy turned down the alley.

He walked with one hand in his pocket, his head slightly back, kicking stones as he went. He was a noisy boy and Artie could hear him muttering as he passed beneath the window. Or maybe he was singing. Artie could see the straight white part in the boy's black hair. He did not think he knew the boy. The house was silent now, and he could not remember why he'd come into the kitchen.

"I saw a cat," he called down. The boy stepped back and looked up. His face split into a wide-open smile.

"Hey, Artie! How're you doin'?"

So he *did* know the boy. How? Who was he? Questions came crawling out of quiet corners to make noise in his head. "It was a yellow cat."

"Yeah, I know. I'm thinking about making a trap for it. Say, why don't you ask your mom if you can come down and help me?"

"I'm sorry, Artie, I didn't hear you. What did you say?" Artie turned just as his mother swung through the kitchen door. She would know the boy. Relieved, he pointed out the window. "There's a boy out there."

"Oh? Let me look." She joined him at the window, waved, and called, "Hello, Kurt. Shouldn't you be in school?"

Artie missed the boy's reply, for in a soft voice his mother told him, "It's Kurt Parks, Artie."

The boy stood shading his eyes with one hand. "Artie and I were just talking. He wants to come down. Would it be okay?"

"I'm afraid not, Kurt," said his mother. "Artie has a doctor's appointment in a short while, and he hasn't found his shoes yet."

"Oh." The boy rocked back on his heels. "Can I come up, then? I'll help him look."

"Yes, tell him yes," Artie said, remembering the lost shoes. "I hate lost shoes—I hate them."

His mother hesitated a moment before saying, "All right, Kurt. But just to visit. Artie can find his own shoes."

Dismayed, Artie cried, "But I want him to help—I can't find them. I can't!"

His mother put an arm around his shoulder, leading him into the living room. "Artie, try to remember where shoes belong. That's the place you need to look."

He hated this game, the looking game. He felt the crashing inside now, fighting and churning. "I looked. Just now. In the kitchen, Mom. I *did* look."

"Honey, think about the things that go in the kitchen. Dishes and pots and food and . . ."

"Drinks," he said, and felt less worried when she smiled.

"Yes, Artie, and drinks. But not shoes."

"I don't know, I don't," he complained over the ring of the bell.

"That'll be Kurt. You two can visit, and then when he's gone, we'll talk about where shoes go."

It was hard, though, once the dark noise began, to silence it. He looked at the boy coming toward him, then grew hopeful again. "I'm looking for my shoes."

His mother patted his arm. "Why don't you take Kurt into your room? Maybe he'd like to see the baseball cards Dad gave you."

Why did she do that? Start another thing when he was trying hard to hang on to the first? He set his teeth and thought, *Shoes. Freakin' shoes.*

"Are you collecting them?" the boy asked.

"Yes," said his mother.

Collecting shoes? Clown words. Artie started to laugh, but his mother gave her head a little shake and his laughter dissolved. Forget clown words. *Shoes. Shoes* were the thing.

"Have you got any good ones, Artie?" the boy asked, leading the way to Artie's bedroom. Artie sat down on the bed and watched the boy move around his room, examining the trophies on his dresser, the long ago pictures of him playing baseball, basketball, riding his bike.

"I used to have a great collection. My dad sent it to me. But then one night my mom was talking on the phone and the grease got too hot on the stove, and all at once there was this awful crackling sound and the whole kitchen was on fire. My baseball card collection was in there and it burned to ashes. All but my Mickey Mantle."

He dropped his voice, and his green eyes, framed by red-rimmed lids and short lashes, were open wide, unblinking and earnest. "It was the weirdest thing. His face, right at the center of the card, was burned. Just the top layer of paper. But the rest of the card was perfect. It didn't even smell smoky. I put it in an envelope, and a long time later, maybe a week after my dad's funeral, I found it. And you know what? The face was back. Only it wasn't Mickey Mantle's face, it was my dad's. Honest to God, it was!"

The boy blinked an honest, wide-eyed blink and looked around the room again. "Man, I haven't been up here in a long time. Where's your electric train stuff?"

Shoes, thought Artie, the boy's words rushing past his ear. *Shoes. Shoes. Shoes.* "Do you think they're under the bed?"

The boy dropped to his knees and lifted the spread. "Nope. There's nothing here but a pair of shoes."

Found! Artie made a grab for them. Short shoes. No strings. His heart plummeted. "These aren't mine."

"Are you sure? They look like they'd fit."

Artie pushed them away. He sat on the bed and hacked at his ankle. "My shoes come up to here. Up to here."

"High-tops? Yeah, well, maybe they're in the closet." The boy dashed across the room and jerked open the door of the walk-in closet.

Help, good help. But it was his own job to look. Artie followed him into the closet and got down on his knees. "They'd be on the floor—shoes belong on the floor."

"Yeah, right," said the boy, and he laughed.

The door swung partway shut, cutting off the light. How could they look with all these dark clothes hanging over them? A match! Yes. "We need a match."

"Why don't we just turn on the . . . hey, yeah. A match! That's cool. Hang on." The boy rose on his knees, worked one hand into his pocket, and came out with a book of matches.

He struck one and passed it to Artie. It didn't give much light. Artie dropped down on his forearms, holding the tiny flame close to the carpet. The smoke curled up his nostrils, and the flame licked at his fingers. Hot. Burning! He dropped the match, sucking his fingers. What was left of the match curled and blackened on the floor.

Suddenly the door swung open. Light flooded the closet, and a foot came down, grinding the match into ashes. "What on earth are you boys doing?"

Looking up at the displeasure on his mother's face, Artie's stomach churned. "Looking for my shoes, Mom."

But his mother had turned her frown away, facing the other boy. She held out her hand. "Give me the matches, Kurt."

Kurt backed out of the closet with a cautious laugh. "It was Artie's idea," he said.

"We'll talk about that in a moment. Artie, your shoes are here by your bed. Put them on, please. Kurt, come with me."

"Sure," said Kurt. He grinned, cocked his nose in the air, and followed Artie's mother out of the room.

He knew that tone. Artie clenched sweaty fists, sounds crashing in his head. His mother was angry. But why? And why did she say those were his shoes when they were not?

He opened the door of his room to tell her, but words were drifting down the hallway. Words about him.

"Artie's judgment isn't always what it ought to be, Kurt. I know you want to be his friend, and I appreciate that. He needs friends now. He's had a rough time."

"I didn't know he was so mixed up about stuff. Honest, I didn't. I thought we were just having a little fun," said the boy.

"Well, now you know," said his mother. "And if you're going to visit him, you have to understand that things aren't like they were when you were friends before. To be Artie's friend now, you'll need maturity and a sense of responsibility. Do you understand what I'm saying?"

"Yeah, I understand."

"No more matches?"

"No."

"I've never been more serious, Kurt," she added over the boy's swift promise. "Artie's like a child in many ways. He can't handle things you take for granted. We're all hoping he'll get better. But in the meantime, we have to be very careful with him. What I'm asking you is, Can you promise to help protect him? Because otherwise I can't leave you two alone together."

"I'll help him," said the boy quickly. "Really, Mrs. Stephens. You can count on me."

Artie crept back to his room and closed the door. In his mind, there were doors closing, too. Slamming hard. Closing him out. He was helpless to stop them. His stomach boiled. He picked up the shoes, the strange shoes, and one after the other flung them at the closed door.

Chapter 17

"Is that you, Coze?" Cozy's mother called from the kitchen.

Cozy dropped her school bag on the sofa and headed for the kitchen. She smiled at the bright-eyed little girl on her mother's lap. "Who's this?"

"Natalie Harper's daughter, Millie. You remember my mentioning Natalie, don't you? She's a friend from Heads Up."

Yeah, right. The support group her mother'd been attending. Natalie was the one with a daughter who'd suffered injuries similar to Artie's. She'd lost a leg, too, if Cozy remembered correctly. Although obviously that was not the girl in her mother's lap.

"Millie, this is Artie's big sister, Cozy," her mother was saying.

Millie slid to her feet and stared at Cozy. "Know what? *My* big sister's getting a new leg today."

Her mother patted Millie's pink cheek. "Millie's staying all night. Won't that be nice?"

"It will come up to here." Millie chopped at her own

short leg several inches below the knee. "Mattie gets a new foot, too. She can do sports. Mattie loves sports. I'm going to be good at sports, too—Mattie says so."

"I bet you will." Cozy caught her mother's eye and grinned.

"Know what else? I'm staying all night!"

"Sleeping in the bathtub, are you?" Cozy teased.

"No, not me."

Cozy laughed and offered, "You can sleep with me, if you want to. As long as you don't snore."

The little girl covered her mouth and giggled. Cozy's mother smiled down at them from the top of a stepstool. "Now that you've worked that out, how about handing me that plastic container?"

Cozy peeled back the lid before handing up the square container. "Matches?"

"We're going to keep them out of reach for a while."

Thinking it had to do with four-year-old fingers, Cozy asked, "How long's Millie staying?"

"Today and tomorrow. Natalie took Mattie to be fitted for a new prosthesis."

Millie nodded and added importantly, "A new leg. See? I told you."

Not anxious to hear any further details, Cozy led the way to the window and pointed to the alley below. "See that cat? He's been living down there."

"Can we pet him?"

"I'm not sure he'll let us. But we can feed him if you'd like. Watch him while I get some milk."

"Pour from the out-of-date carton." Cozy's mother came down off the chair.

"Where's Artie?"

"He has an appointment with the rehab psychologist."

"Dad took him?"

"He had to agree that with Millie along, I'd have had my hands full. How was school?" her mother asked in the next breath, the defensiveness in her voice disappearing as abruptly as it had surfaced.

"The usual. Except for an unscheduled fire drill in study hall, thanks to Kurt Parks. He brought an electric buzzer of some kind, and it sounded just like the fire bell." Cozy grinned in spite of herself. "The principal gave him the rest of the day off for bad behavior."

"That explains it, then," said her mother.

"Explains what?"

"He was here today."

"Kurt Parks? Are you serious? What for?"

"Artie saw him from the window. They exchanged a few words, and Kurt invited himself up."

"And you let him come in?" Cozy demanded.

Her mother turned on the tap, filled a cup with water, and put it in the microwave. Reaching for a tea bag, she said quietly, "Artie could use a few friends, you know."

"Artie's got friends. Biff and Alfonzo and Marcus and . . ."

"And where are they all?"

In the following silence, Cozy realized her mom had a point. Biff hadn't been to see Artie since that awful time in the hospital. None of his other friends had, either. Lamely, she said, "I don't know, but Kurt's a pain, Mom. And a weasel. Artie won't know enough not to trust him."

"Cozy, I'm not giving Kurt free rein. I just think it'll do Artie good to have someone his own age around."

"He's got me . . . and Star."

"Yes, you've both been wonderful. But he needs male friends, too. I explained the situation to Kurt. He seems to want to help."

"But Mom—he lies!"

"I know that. . . ." She drew a deep breath, took her cup from the microwave, and set it down so sharply that the water sloshed and made a damp ring on the tablecloth. "But Artie made the first move when he called out the window to Kurt. We have to respect that."

"Know what?" said Millie, trying to steal back the show. "Mattie's going to play tennis on her new leg."

But Cozy wasn't listening.

Chapter 18

The little girl asked too many questions. Artie's ears had had enough. He stretched out on the sofa and heard his mother whisper,

"Let's go out in the kitchen and color a picture."

The little girl asked, "Did his extracises make him tired?"

"Perhaps they did," said his mother.

"I'm not tired. I don't take naps."

"No, I didn't suppose so," said his mother.

Artie closed his eyes. The little girl's voice grew dimmer and dimmer until he could no longer hear it. But then the doorbell woke him. And another voice—a boy's voice, said, "I thought, if you didn't care, I'd take Artie for a walk."

His mother asked, "Shouldn't you be in school?"

"There was a fire in shop, so they let us out early."

"A fire? Cozy hasn't come home," his mother said suspiciously.

"Just the kids in shop class, I mean. It was a little fire, see, and they got it out right away. . . . But it was kind of messy, so they—"

"Mmm," Artie's mother cut short the boy's words. But the boy started up again.

"The cat's in the alley. Can Artie come with me to see it?"

"I'm afraid Artie's asleep."

"No, I'm not." Artie swung his feet to the floor and sat up so fast his head whirled—worried that the boy would get away. "Who is it, Mom? Who is it?"

"It's Kurt Parks, Artie," she said, stepping aside. The door opened all the way. A tall, black-haired boy with a round face and red, itchy-looking eyelids grinned and waved.

"Hi, Artie."

"Hi." It was familiar, this face, like a pale picture in Artie's mind. He cocked his head to one side and chewed the inside of his lip, trying to remember.

"Do you want to come see the cat?" the boy asked.

Artie got right to his feet. But his mother was shaking her head. "I'm sorry, Kurt, but he can't right now. Maybe later, when Cozy's home."

"Oh," said the boy. He kept smiling, but it looked out of tilt on his face. "Another time, I guess."

"Yes, another time," said his mother. But the boy still didn't move, and she couldn't close the door. So she said, "As long as you're here, would you like to come in?"

The boy's smile became real again. He walked to the sofa and sat down. Artie sat down, too.

"I saw the signs in the hall. Did your neighbor hang them, or you?"

STOP and YIELD and ONE WAY flashed in his mind. Confused, Artie looked at his mother.

"Artie sometimes runs ahead and rings Mrs. Harding's doorbell instead of ours," she explained. "It makes her dog bark, and that upsets her, so we thought signs would help Artie remember. I don't think she means to be difficult. She's just not very well."

A loud crash from the kitchen made Artie jump. His mother called, "Millie! Are you all right?" and hurried off to see what was happening.

"I'll take those signs down if you want me to," said the boy when they were alone. "It doesn't matter, anyway, about ringing Harding's bell, 'cause the cheese done slid off that old woman's cracker."

Clown words! Artie burst out laughing. It felt good in his belly, to laugh. Light and ticklish and sunny.

"Loony tunes, that's what she is," said the boy.

Artie didn't know the word, but he kept on laughing, since the boy was laughing, too.

The boy slid a little closer and said, "Remember when we used to ring Mrs. Harding's bell and run?" He laughed and lowered his voice even further. "I call her sometimes. She says 'Hello?' and I say, 'Mrs. Harding?' Then she says, 'Yes?' and I say, 'What did you want?' She gets flustered and stammers and . . ." The boy turned.

Artie turned, too. It was the little girl with the yellow hair. She looked at the boy with lively interest and said, "I spilled the pans."

"You must be Millie," said the boy.

Up and down went her head. She came closer, then said, "Know what? My sister's getting a new leg."

"Oh, yeah?" said the boy.

She edged still closer, poking her toe in the carpet. "Does your leg come off?"

Artie looked down at his legs. He pinched the skin beneath his pants leg and shook his head.

"Not you, him," said the girl, pointing to Kurt.

"No, but my father's does. It's a real special leg, too. It's computerized. If he pulls up his pants leg, he can get the time, the temperature, and the balance in his checking account. Honest!" he added, his eyes wide and unblinking.

His words came too fast. Artie's nerves twanged as he tried to follow. The little girl said, "You're silly."

"Yeah? Well, you're Millie." The boy hooted, his laughter booming off the walls.

Artie laughed, too, and the little girl giggled. She sat down in the chair facing them. The boy turned to Artie. "Did I tell you, I think I'm going to trap that cat?"

"What for?" asked the little girl.

"Because he's a nice kitty," said the boy, winking at Artie.

"Cozy and I feed him," said the girl.

"Have you got a piece of paper, Artie? We could draw a plan for the trap."

"What's a trap?" asked the girl.

"It's a cat house," said the boy, winking again.

A cat house? A cat house! For a cat. To hold and pet and play with. The thought of it made Artie warm inside. *Cat*, he thought. Remember. Must remember. And this boy. He must remember him, too. Two Must-Remembers. He opened one hand and thought, *Cat*, then closed it tight. He opened the other and thought, *Boy*, then closed it tight, too. Two Must-Remembers.

Chapter 19

Cozy could see Mrs. Harding's door from the elevator, with the sign: ONE MORE DOOR, ARTIE.

She had her hand on the knob of the door marked ARTIE LIVES HERE, when it opened and Kurt Parks came strolling out of the apartment as if he lived there.

"I beat you home," he said, grinning as if they were the best of friends. "There was a fire in—"

"Yeah, right."

She swept past him, closed the door behind her, and headed for the bathroom. There was a sign there, too, up over the toilet. ARTIE, PLEASE LIFT THE RIM, it read. There were some lifelong habits Artie didn't need reminding of, like washing his hands before eating, or remembering which chair was his, or always asking for the front seat. Probably, Cozy thought, as she dried it off once again, he'd never really been very good about lifting the rim—just a better aim.

When she came out, Millie was waiting, full of excitement about the cat house that Artie and "that boy" were planning to build. Artie smiled and nodded as Millie ran on. It was a typically nutty Kurt Parks idea, but she didn't spoil it for them by asking how they planned to make a wild tomcat sleep in a pet house.

Natalie Harper came by for Millie, and they all went into the kitchen. Millie danced from foot to foot, trying to squeeze into half a minute an account of the past two days. Natalie laughed and hugged her, asking, "Did she wear out your ears, Artie?"

Artie made no reply, but turned his head to one side and looked back at her. She had deep-set eyes that were kind and patient. Natalie waited. "You're pretty," he said finally.

Natalie smiled. "What a nice compliment. Thank you, Artie."

Noting her mother's disconcerted expression, Cozy hid her own blush behind a cupboard door. When Millie saw her open the cupboard, she smacked her lips and called for cookies. Cozy took out the cookies and closed the cupboard door.

"A picnic, a picnic, let's have a picnic," Millie sang, tracking Cozy from cupboard to refrigerator and back again.

Humoring her, Cozy poured three glasses of juice, then added string cheese and the package of cookies to the tray, while her mother fixed coffee for herself and Natalie. Artie and Millie trailed after Cozy into the living room, where she spread an afghan on the floor to make the picnic official.

Chapter 20

The picture on the cookie package made Artie's mouth water. It seemed to him that it took Cozy a long time to open the package. She offered it to the little girl first. Then she took two herself. He plunged his hand forward and in his eagerness felt the cookies crumble. The crumbs on his fingertips and the delicious chocolate aroma as he inhaled made his nose tingle.

"Wait a second, Artie. You're smashing them!" Cozy cried.

But he could not stop himself. He pulled his hand free of the package and pushed and pushed the cookies into his mouth, until there was no more space. They scratched the roof of his mouth, rubbed against the back of his throat, and soaked the moisture out of his tongue.

"Slow down, Artie! You're going to choke," Cozy warned.

"Piggy, piggy," said the little girl with the yellow hair. She covered her mouth and giggled. Suddenly, Artie felt ashamed. Heat spread from the roots of his hair through his scalp to his skull and down his face and neck. Unable to look at the little girl, or Cozy, he brushed the crumbs from his hands. Some of them slid off his lap onto the afghan, getting lost in the loops.

Cozy touched his arm, saying, "You want some cheese, don't you, Artie?"

He looked at the tray. Cheese? Is that what it was? It looked like short, pale sticks. He could not think how you ate short, pale sticks. And the little girl was watching him. Watching to see if he'd make another mistake. She was so busy watching him that she knocked over her glass of juice.

"Run into the kitchen and grab a dish towel," Cozy told her.

Artie was glad when she was gone. Maybe he could ask Cozy how to eat the cheese. But, no, he didn't want to do that, not if it was something he should know. He would just watch and see how she ate hers. Patiently he waited. But her fingers did not reach for the cheese. She was looking at him with a look that pulled her eyebrows close together. Softly she said, "Artie, remember when we were in the kitchen and you told Mrs. Harper she was pretty?"

"The little girl's mother?"

Cozy nodded.

It puzzled him, her embarrassment. He chewed the inside of his lip. "She is. She is pretty, Cozy."

"I know. I think so, too. But she's a grown-up. So you shouldn't say that to her. You could say her dress was pretty. That would be fine," she added. "But you shouldn't come right out and say, 'You're pretty.' "

Another mistake! There had been no clues, nothing on the screen in his head, no grinding twinges in his stomach. You had to be so careful. Even true things you sometimes couldn't say. Not out loud, anyway. He suspected the other boy had known—that other boy he had been.

His head hummed with a distant thunder that grew louder and louder, until the noise ran together like a room full of laughing people. Different laughs. All laughing at him. At his mistakes.

His vision blurred, but he would not give in to it. Tilt, he thought. Tilt. He drew a deep breath and let it go. Drew another. Unclenched his fists, one hand, then the other.

Chapter 21

Cozy scribbled down her English assignment, suspecting that Micah Daniels was watching her. It was a week ago that he'd brought the pizza. Since then, he'd talked to her after class several days in a row. The prom was coming up. Maybe he'd ask her, but then again, maybe he wouldn't. She wasn't sure the prom was his kind of thing.

Only a few minutes before the bell, Mrs. Ballard began to read aloud the descriptive paragraphs that had been assigned the previous week. One described aged toenails, another a woman ironing a T-shirt, ironing it and ironing it, until the decal stuck to the bottom of the iron. It had a kind of haunting quality. And the next . . . Cozy's stomach jerked as she heard familiar words. . . .

The coughs, paper ripping, and clatter of shoes on chair rungs died away. Even the dependably boisterous students grew attentive as Mrs. Ballard read the paper Cozy had written, describing the emergency room at the hospital as the family waited to hear about Artie. Although it was less than five hundred words, it seemed to go on and on.

Mrs. Ballard finally lay the paper aside. "As you'll recall, I asked for five senses. This paper has given us a sixth.

Emotion has a pulse beat all its own. And what emotion does this piece of writing evoke?"

"Fear."

Cozy twisted around and met Micah Daniels's gray eyes. He jerked up a thumb and whispered, "Good job."

Mercifully, the bell rang, eliminating further discussion. Cozy collected her belongings and filed out into the corridor. She used to like school. Now even English was an ordeal.

"Wait up a second. I want to tell you something," Micah called after her.

"The cafeteria's on fire, and we can all go home?"

He sniffed and then grinned. "No, I think that's lunch cooking. But if you feel that way about it, let's ditch school for the rest of the day."

"I don't think so."

"No guts," he accused.

"I guess not," she agreed, and sneaked another glance at his misaligned nose. There was a scar just over his upper lip, another on his chin, and a third teardrop-shaped one at the corner of his left eye. But they were clear, intelligent eyes.

"You've got a pretty good fix on hospitals," he said, after a silence that stretched half the length of the corridor.

"How did you know the description was mine?" Cozy asked.

"Psychic powers."

"Not likely."

"Deductive reasoning?"

"Meaning?"

He shrugged. "She read one of your papers last week. You're the only one in there who can write with any depth."

"She read three."

"One puddle, one pond, and one with depth. It had to be yours."

"You're full of it, too," Cozy said, and he laughed.

"All right, so I've got good eyes. I saw your title when you handed it in."

Cozy asked, "So what'd you write about? Toenails?"

"Isn't that what she pleads for? Creativity?"

He grinned, and she noticed the fullness of his bottom lip, how it lifted at the corners. His hair, walnut brown, wavy and thick, brushed his collar as he turned to add, "I liked what you wrote. You told it just right."

Flustered, Cozy hugged her books and kept walking.

He kept pace with her, asking, after a moment's hesitation, "How's your brother?"

"He's making progress, slow but sure."

"That's what Kurt Parks said. He must stop by a lot, huh?"

Cozy shrugged. "No one invites him—he just comes."

He looked off down the corridor, a muscle along his jawline twitching. "Is there something going on between you two?"

"Kurt Parks? Are you kidding! The guy's a nut!"

He held up his hands as if to fend off a blow. "Just asking. I'm new here, remember?"

Cozy grinned in spite of herself. "Just don't start any rumors."

"If I was into rumors, I could do better than that." He smiled and left, turning back to give her a wave. "See you."

When Cozy walked home from school, she was still thinking about Micah. She found a note from her mother saying Artie had an appointment with the rehab psychologist and they'd be late getting back.

Cozy was finishing up her homework when her father came home. At dinnertime her mother and Artie still hadn't returned, so they went to work on a pizza.

Cozy found the pan and the vegetable oil while her father gathered the makings from the refrigerator shelves. She slid a knife into the seam of the cardboard tube, but on seeing the perforated lines in the dough stopped short. "Oh oh. We've got a problem here, Dad."

He indicated the instructions on the tube. "Nothing to it. Just fit it to the cookie sheet and you've got a pizza crust. See here, it says—"

"It says 'breadsticks.' "

He pushed at the refrigerated dough, straightened his glasses, and frowned at the perforated lines. "So it is. Now what?"

"Breadsticks, I guess. Unless you know how to make homemade pizza crust."

So they lined the bottom of a cookie sheet with flattened-out breadsticks and poured on the pizza sauce, the toppings, and plenty of cheese. They watched it bake, laughing and making up pizza-stick jokes.

Everything was ready but the table when Artie announced his arrival home with a long ring on the doorbell. His father went to let them in but returned to the kitchen a moment later. The pleasure of the comedy pizza was gone from his face. Cozy's stomach tightened.

"What's the matter?"

"Artie rang Mrs. Harding's bell again. Your mother's in the hallway, smoothing it over."

Cozy winced. "I guess the notes didn't help."

"Maybe he didn't read them." Her father passed his hand over his face.

Chapter 22

Artie stood just inside the door, his shoulders hunched, his hands clamped over his ears. But he couldn't block out the shrill yipping of the dog, the harsh voice that belonged to the woman, or his mother's voice. The noise in the hall was his fault. He had rung the wrong bell, the wrong freakin' bell.

Crazy. The word crashed across his mind.

It wasn't a clown word. It had sharp points.

Had the woman called him that? Or was the message his own?

He did not want to be crazy. He tried hard not to be.

But he was afraid of it. Lost words. Lost skills. Lost objects. Lost days and weeks and months. Crazy, freakin' crazy.

He could not stop trembling. His chest felt hot and swollen, with his heart pounding against the tightness. He could feel sobs pushing upward, making his throat thick with tears. But when he opened his mouth, laughter spilled out. It terrified him, the laughter mingled with tears. He clenched his fists, his jaw. He squeezed at the laughter, tighter and tighter until he shut it off, letting the tears fall alone.

His father came out of the kitchen and caught him with the tears streaming down his face. "I-I c-c-can't help it. I c-can't," he sobbed.

"Artie, take it easy. It's okay," his father said, coming to him. "So you rang the wrong bell. It's not the end of the world. It's okay."

Artie heard the reassurances and felt his father's arm around his shoulder. But through his tears he also saw the flush on his father's cheeks and the awkward way he averted his eyes. It confused Artie.

"It's okay?"

"Sure, it is. Your mom's taking care of it. Come on, now. Let's get changed and wash up for dinner."

Artie nodded and started for his room. But he looked down at his shoes, the odd shoes that didn't seem right for his feet, and he knew that everything was *not* okay. If everything were okay, he wouldn't be wearing someone else's shoes.

In his mind was the dim shadow of another boy, a boy in white sneakers with stubby laces, who'd made his father proud. What had happened to that boy? Where was he now?

Chapter 23

"Mom said you can choose the fruit. Apples, bananas, or strawberries?" Cozy said as they crossed at the light and walked on toward the produce stand at the corner of the Colonial Plaza parking lot.

Artie was singing inside, because Cozy's friend Star had come along. It was always more fun when Star came.

"They've got pineapple and oranges, too," she said, in the way that made him feel bold and able to choose.

"Oranges."

"Are you sure?" Cozy asked. "They're kind of messy."

"Oranges, it's oranges, Cozy," Artie said, knowing now that it had to be oranges.

"Okay, but let's wait until we get home to eat them," said Cozy, opening her pocketbook. "You buy them. Star and I'll wait here."

It was paper light, the money. But it made his mind heavy, for he did not know how much oranges were in money. He looked at the man behind the stand. A tall man with a busy face. "You do it, Cozy."

"It isn't difficult, Artie. Just tell the man you have two dollars and you want a bag of oranges."

But what if two dollars was not enough? He shuffled from foot to foot, pulled at his lip, then backed away, careful not to look at Star. "I don't want oranges. I'm not hungry. I'm not hungry at all."

"Oh, come on, Artie. You're always hungry," Cozy said. But she didn't know what the dread of being wrong did to his stomach.

"That's because he's so thin. The boy's positively caved in. Slap two slices of bread on these ribs and you'd have a skinny-bone sandwich."

Star's clown words made him laugh. For a moment, he forgot his dilemma. "Skinny-bone, skinny-bone. That's pretty funny words, huh?"

"For a pretty funny boy. Now about the oranges—one is enough for me." She shoved her hands into the pockets of her jacket and smiled.

It was a good strong smile, full of sunshine and promise. And yet he crumpled the bills in his hand, scuffed his shoe against the pavement. The money—he did not know about money. A saving thought came on like a light. He offered her the money. "You get them, Star. You're our guest. Guests go first."

Cozy looked surprised. Star chuckled. "Be a gentleman, Artie. Go on, get us each one. Get your mother one, too. And your dad. Do it just for me. Please?"

He gazed at her a moment longer, and thought that she looked as if she knew about money—about everything there was to know about anything. But she was asking him, and he could not say that he didn't know how much oranges were in money. So he clenched the money tight in his fist and made his legs go straight to the man.

"Can I help you, son?" His voice sounded faint through the worry in Artie's ears.

"We want oranges. One for me, one for Star, one for Cozy." He turned and pointed at them. The man put three oranges in a sack.

"Wait a second, here's your change," said the man. Artie took that along with the sack. Above the knocking of his heart, he heard the man say, "Thank you. Come back again."

Warm words, friendly words. The sounds in his head quieted. "Okay, we will."

Cozy patted his shoulder. "Good job, Artie. You did very well."

"Well? He did *well?* You won't find a slicker orange-picker in all of Chippewah!" Star said.

"Slicker orange-picker!" Artie threw his head back and laughed as the tight knots in his stomach came free. He offered Star the sack.

"No, you carry them. We'll eat them when we get to your house."

"You're coming, too?"

"Of course I am—you've got the oranges!" she said, and she hugged him. For a moment, it was like a shower of sparks in his head. Then she let go and gave him a Lifesaver, and Cozy got one, too.

He walked between them as they crossed the highway. They did not ask him, as his mother would, if he knew the way back. He was glad, for he knew the buildings as he came to them, but he didn't feel sure of what lay ahead. Not until his eyes reached out and showed him.

There was a note waiting for them on the kitchen table. Cozy read it aloud: "Gone to the library. Put potatoes in to bake. Fix salad. I'll pick up chicken." She tossed the note in the trash and opened one drawer, then another. "I thought we had an orange peeler; one of those little yellow things."

A dismal dread came over Artie. He made himself ask, "Is it lost?"

"If it is, it's not worth looking for."

It was strange, how lost things did not worry Cozy. He watched her jerk the lid off the cookie jar and inhale.

"Mmm. Chocolate chippers. Did you help bake them, Artie?"

"Did I?" It alarmed him, not knowing. He took a cookie and pushed the whole thing into his mouth. He reached for another, crammed it in, too, and had his hand in the jar again when he remembered—Mom sweeping up flour as he ate cookie batter out of the bowl. "That's right, I did! I helped Mom make the cookies."

"Mmm, good. Have one, Star," said Cozy, cutting the oranges in half.

The juice drops made Artie's mouth water. He sank his teeth through the pulp, tasted the sweetness on his tongue.

Cozy wiped off the table and said, "Oprah's on."

He glanced at the clock, trying to remember if the hands were where they should be when Oprah came on. But he couldn't. So he trusted Cozy's certainty and started for the living room.

Star asked, "You like Oprah?"

Artie nodded, and after a moment's hesitation told her his discovery: " 'Oprah.' That's 'harpo' backwards—did you know?"

Star rolled her eyes upward, as if she, too, had a screen in her head, then wrote out the letters in the air. "Hey, it is! That's pretty sharp, Artie."

A comforting warmth spread through him. He asked, "Do you like Oprah, too?"

"I don't watch her very often."

"You should. She's pretty, Star. And she's nice."

"You think so? Well, maybe we should check it out. Coze, are you coming?"

Cozy turned on the tap and rinsed her hands. "I'd better put the potatoes in and make the salad first."

Chapter 24

Artie turned on the TV. He sat on the floor, with his back against the sofa. Star dropped to the floor, too. She set a plate with what was left of the oranges and cookies between them, asking, "Which channel?"

"I'll get it," Artie said. But his fingers were sticky, and he had trouble with the remote control.

"Want me to help?" Star asked.

"I can do it." His heartbeat quickened. He was anxious not to fail. He pushed one button and then another. Oprah came on the screen. The accomplishment gave him a spurt of pleasure. He pointed, saying, "See, that's Oprah!"

"So it is," Star said, grinning.

Oprah was talking in her voice that made him think of deep water. Calm and strong. She had eyes that understood things. "Are you there, caller?" she said.

"I'm going to call her," Artie told Star.

"Do you know the number?"

Should he? It worried him, not knowing. "I probably won't call her today. Not while you're here."

Star bit into an orange. The juice squirted out and caught

him in the eye, burning. She tossed her head, laughing. "Oops! I got you. Sorry, Artie."

Artie rubbed his eye, but the dried juice on his fingers made it burn all the more.

"Here." Star took off her jacket. She used a piece of the sleeve to rub his smarting eye. She smelled like oranges. A strand of hair stuck to the juice on her chin.

He thought about her hair, how soft and pretty it was.

"Better?" she asked, and he nodded.

She settled back against the sofa again, watching TV. But he kept looking at her. Her shirt was the same color as the orange. The way that it fit made him aware of her breasts. They pressed from the inside of her shirt, round and firm.

"Is something wrong?" she asked.

He started to tell her she was pretty, then stopped. His stomach felt tight; there was heat in him, too. It confused him, because he could not think why it would be wrong to tell her. But it was so hard to know. So much gray fuzz. There was nothing but static on the space in his head. His stomach often gave him warnings his mind did not. He looked down at his shoes, the velcro straps.

She reached for another orange. "You aren't watching. I thought you *liked* Oprah."

"I do. But I like you better."

"You sweet talker, you," she said, and laughed again.

Her laughter released the knot in his stomach. He laughed, too, and went on noticing things: her slim legs, crossed at the ankles, her hair spilling over one shoulder, trailing down to her breast, and clinging to the shirt that moved with her when she breathed. She kept rotating the orange half in her hand, working her way around it with her teeth. Then she turned the skin inside out and twirled it on her finger.

"Looks kind of like an umbrella, don't you think?"

"It looks like this," Artie said, reaching out and putting his hand over her breast.

Star leaped to her feet, spilling orange skins and cookies, and yelled, "Artie Stephens, don't you ever do that again!"

All the warmth and contentment, the mounting excitement, collapsed. Heat, noise, bewildering confusion screamed through his skull. She was still talking, her eyes flashing, her mouth drawn down, angry words that he could not hear for the chaos inside him. On the screen in his head, the jeering crowd roared, pointed fingers, tittering, chortling, guffawing.

Tears and the laughter spilled out of him all at once. Wrong laughter. Miswired laughter. "I'm sorry, I'm sorry," he said through ragged laughing sobs. He drew his knees to his chest, buried his face against them, hugged himself in a tight ball, and squeezed tighter, tighter until finally the laughter stopped, leaving only the tears.

When he found the courage to lift his head, he was alone. He looked at the mess on the floor: the upside-down plate, the orange skins, the cookies. He tried to stop trembling, stop crying. From far, far away, he heard a calm, deep voice:

"Are you there, caller?"

It was Oprah. She was still on the television. She had her hand to her ear and blinked, waiting.

"I'm here—it's me, Artie," he said.

But Oprah didn't answer him. No one wanted to talk to a crazy boy. Not Oprah. Not Star. Fresh tears swelled in his throat. He wiped his nose on his sleeve and wished he could be that other boy again.

Latching his arms around his knees again, Artie rocked against the sofa, forward and back, forward and back, crying and wishing.

Chapter 25

"I tried to call you last night," Cozy said, as she and Star left school under an overcast sky.

"Couldn't get through, could you? Between Mom and my sisters, I'm lucky to get ten minutes a week on the phone."

It was a common complaint of Star's. Cozy scarcely listened. She was tense, and had been since yesterday when Star left without saying good-bye. Cozy hadn't slept well, puzzling over the strangeness of it. And Artie. He'd thumped the wall with his foot and ground his teeth enough to raise the dead. Having waited for this moment alone, Cozy was now hesitant to ask. She glanced sidelong at Star.

"So what happened yesterday?"

"Happened?"

"By the time I finished in the kitchen, you were gone."

Star hunted in her purse for Lifesavers. "Yeah, well, I got to thinking about it being the day they deliver the bottled water and how I was supposed to be home by four to let the guy in. Split-second panic."

"You didn't even say good-bye."

"Yes, I did, Cozy. I hollered to you. Maybe you didn't hear me. You had that food processor going."

She *had* shredded vegetables for the salad. And the thing made an awful racket. Off in the distance, thunder rumbled. "We'd better hurry or we're going to get wet. You're coming home with me, aren't you?" Cozy asked.

"I can't today. I've got to baby-sit, remember?"

They parted company a few minutes later. The first raindrops fell on Cozy's cheeks just before she reached her building. She glanced down the alley and saw the yellow cat dash for cover. The scraps she'd put out for it that morning were gone. A sudden gust of wind picked up the flimsy aluminum dish and skipped it down the alley.

Cozy's mother left for the library as soon as Cozy got home. Artie was listless, not interested in doing anything more strenuous than pushing buttons on the remote control. Cozy started on her homework. She was halfway through her English when Kurt Parks rang the doorbell.

He was rain-splattered, dark hair plastered to his head. Cozy backed away a step as he sneezed and wiped his watery eyes. "Can I talk to Artie a minute?"

"We can't have company when Mom's not home."

"Star was here yesterday."

"Star's an exception."

"Oh."

He smiled the same bland smile, as if he thought he could smile his way in. She began closing the door. "Good-bye, Kurt."

"Tell Artie I'll be back later," he called through the shrinking crack.

Cozy returned to her English, thinking fleetingly of Micah. It made her face burn to think he'd mistaken Kurt's dogged interest in Artie for interest in her.

Oprah was over when the doorbell rang again. Cozy let

her father in. Kurt rushed off the elevator and hurried to catch up.

"Hi, Mr. Stephens. I wanted to show these to Artie." The dusty pieces of scrap lumber made wet dirty streaks against his shirt.

Her father smiled a tired smile. "I heard you boys were going to do some building."

"A house for a cat you can't even catch. Sure." Cozy rolled her eyes.

Her father gave her a hard look and beckoned to Kurt. "Artie? You've got company."

Artie's face brightened. He rolled off the sofa and onto his feet. "Can you stay?"

"For a while." Kurt sailed past Cozy with his never-failing smile. Fuming, she started after her father. On the threshhold of the kitchen, he swung around, nearly trampling her toes.

"You boys put some newspaper under those boards. I'll look for a saw and help you cut them to size." The kitchen door swung shut behind them. He looked back, asking, "Is it my imagination, or are you following me?"

"This isn't the way to get rid of Kurt."

"Does Artie *want* to get rid of him?"

"Artie doesn't know any better!"

He arched an eyebrow, and she blushed, feeling somehow that he'd scored an unfair point. "I don't get it! A few years ago, you were the first one to point out Kurt Parks was a pain."

Her father chuckled. "He's grown up a little since then." He leaned against the counter and scratched his chin, asking, "What's this kid done to be so unpopular with you?"

"Give me a break, Dad. I shouldn't have to explain this to you."

"Just this once?" He grinned.

She sighed and stared glumly back at him. He patted her on the head like she was a little kid. "I know you're concerned about Artie. But there's a difference between being a caretaker and a jailor. Think about it."

Her indignation rose, but before she could formulate a response, he took a handsaw from his toolbox on the bottom shelf of the pantry and went back into the living room.

Cozy stayed in the kitchen, smarting from the gentle reproof. She could hear the murmur of voices, Kurt's cattle-call laughter, Artie's questions, and eventually the hesitant, irregular squawks of the saw being applied to the wood by amateur hands.

Chapter 26

"Take another look at the map, Artie," his mother was saying.

"Artie?" his mother gently prodded.

He turned his eyes back to the monitor. There was a colored picture of a map. The map was of a town, but it wasn't Chippewah. It was a different town. The Lost Town, he thought.

"Now, remember, this is the school. It is on School Street. Study the map closely. Let's say you lived on Maple Street. Show me how you would walk to school. How would you get to 710 School Street from 101 North Maple?"

Why *wasn't* he at school?

He looked at the calendar. It was turned to May. Wasn't May a school month? Was Cozy at school? Was Star?

"What day is it?" he asked finally.

"Artie, honey. Look at the map," his mother said.

"I want to know what day it is."

"It's Wednesday, the second day of May," his mother said. "Why?"

She looked at him closely. His palms grew moist, his pulse began to race, his head hummed. Something was wrong with his question. Wrong questions had razor-sharp points. They turned on the asker. "Never mind."

"Did you have a question about it?"

Artie shook his head.

"About therapy, maybe?"

"No."

"We should have gone to therapy today. But the washing machine ran over, remember? We had to wait for the man to come fix it," his mother said. "Is that what you were wondering about?"

He hesitated a long moment, then nodded. She looked pleased. He felt weak—he'd come so close to asking the wrong question.

"Look at the map now and show me the best route to school."

He looked at the monitor. He saw 101 North Maple Street. He saw the school. He could read a map. This part was not too difficult. All he had to do was think about it.

"Go to the corner . . ."

"That's the candy store," his mother pointed out. "Remember?"

He nodded.

"Are you looking for landmarks?"

He nodded again.

"What do you do at the corner?"

"Turn and walk straight to the school."

"Which way do you turn at the candy store?"

"Left."

"Very good, Artie. Ready for the close-up?"

Her words were growing softer, blending together, slipping away. His eyes wandered to the calendar again.

"Artie? Look at the monitor. Use the space bar to move along. Okay. Find your way to school."

The picture on the monitor had changed. The map was gone. It was a street now. There were houses along the street. There was a boy on the sidewalk in front of one house.

"Do you have a picture of the map in your head? Can you see how to get to school? Push the space bar to start moving. Now! You're at the end of the sidewalk. Do you want to turn?"

Artie didn't know. He just didn't know. He looked at the space in his head, but the map wasn't there. Why couldn't he keep the freakin' map in his head?

"Artie," his mother began.

"I know, I know." He held his thumb down on the space bar just to keep her from talking. The boy skipped along on choppy little steps. Cozy came in and asked him what he was working on, but he didn't know. So he looked down at the keys, pretending he didn't hear her question.

"He's trying to get to school. He made it to the candy store—isn't that great?" said his mother.

"Great," Cozy said. "Did you bring me a Hershey Bar, Artie?"

He took his fingers off the space bar, turning to look at her. She knew there was no real candy store in the computer. Why would she ask a dumb question like that?

She grinned at him. "What's the matter? Didn't they have Hersheys? Snickers would have been okay."

Making fun, he thought. Like he was . . . retarded. A glaring word, he hated it. Heat rushed to his face. "It's a game, stupid."

She looked surprised, like his words had scratched her. Looking down at his hands, he heard her ask his mother, "Are you going to the library?"

"No, the Historical Society. I hope I can wrap up my research this time. I might be awhile. Why don't you invite Star over?"

His little finger hit the reset key. The screen cleared, and set the disk drive whirring, resetting the game. "Will she come, Cozy?"

"Sorry, Artie. I already asked her. She can't today."

"I want to tell her something," he said, and then regretted it. He did not want Cozy, or *anyone*, to know what it was he had to say to Star.

"What is it you want to tell her?" his mother asked.

He clamped his jaws together. Looked at the screen. "Something. Just something."

"Something *what*?" Cozy asked.

He looked at his hands, and picked at a scab on his thumb. "I can't tell you. It's a secret."

"I won't tell," Cozy promised.

The scab came free and fell on his trousers. He brushed it onto the floor. He couldn't tell her the mistake he had made, so he said instead, "Her name backwards is 'Rats,' but don't tell, Cozy. I want to tell her. Let me."

Cozy nodded, said, "Maybe she'll come home with me tomorrow. I'll be sure to invite her. Okay?"

"Will she come?"

"I don't know. She's baby-sitting some kids on her street now. I can't promise she'll come."

He frowned. A promise was best. A promise meant for sure. "Why can't you promise?"

"I just told you, Artie, she's got a baby-sitting job."

"That's stupid." There was anger in him, fighting, wanting to get free. He got out of his chair, shoved it up against the desk, and started down the hall.

"Artie?" his mother called after him.

He knew what she wanted; it was always the same. "I know, I know. Lift the rim, lift the freakin' rim." He slammed the bathroom door and pressed his face against it, feeling it tremble.

Chapter 27

Artie stood by the kitchen window. He had a plank of wood in one hand and a piece of sandpaper in the other. When he sanded, he forgot to watch. When he watched, he forgot to sand. He turned as Cozy came in. She had newspapers in her hand.

"You're getting sawdust all over the floor. I'll put these down, and you can work at the table."

"Is Kurt coming?" he asked.

"I don't know, Artie. Maybe he found something else to do today."

Artie tried to think what other things Kurt might be doing. Nothing came.

"Oprah's on," Cozy said.

"I don't want to watch."

"Why not? I thought you liked her."

"I don't want to," he said again.

"All right. I'll be in the other room if you want me."

He was glad to be alone. It was better alone. Not so many things to hear and see and think all at the same time.

The wood had grown heavy in his hand. He put it on

the table and returned to the window just in time to see Kurt picking up the yellow cat. It was like sudden sunlight filling him. He pressed his nose against the screen and called.

"I want to hold him. Can I hold him?"

"It's a *her*," said Kurt. "She's got kittens."

"Oh," Artie said, although it didn't seem quite right. It itched in his mind, but he couldn't reach what was wrong with it.

Kurt tipped back his head and sneezed. Startled, the cat leaped to the ground and disappeared through the open basement window just behind Kurt. Kurt wiped his nose on the sleeve of his jacket. A funny jacket—something was missing.

"That's where she lives, but don't tell," Kurt was saying. "The super doesn't like cats."

"Oh," Artie said, still staring at his jacket.

"Come down, and I'll show you where she hides."

"Okay."

Artie had gotten to the living room when he realized he wasn't wearing shoes. "Where are my shoes?"

Cozy held her finger in the book she was reading. "I don't know, Artie. Wherever you left them, I guess."

"I need them. I'm going downstairs."

"What for?"

"Kurt's down there."

"Artie, you can't go down by yourself."

"Yes, I can," he said, itch-weed turning inside. "I used to," he added, knowing as he said it, that it was that other boy who'd come and gone all by himself.

Cozy's face reddened. "Artie," she said, and she reached out as if to touch him.

But he pulled back, for he didn't want to hear Can't-Do

words; there were so many Can't-Do words. The brightness within dimmed. He turned and went back to the kitchen. Kurt was leaning against the building on the other side of the alley, still wearing the funny jacket.

"I thought you were coming down."

"No."

"Why not?"

He wasn't about to say Cozy wouldn't let him. So he lifted his shoulders and said nothing.

Kurt pushed away from the building. He leaned one hand on his waist and shaded his eyes. "Okay if I come up?"

"Yes, you come up," Artie agreed. When Kurt came into the kitchen, Artie couldn't stop looking at his jacket. It was a brown jacket with a zipper down the front and pockets on the side. But the troublesome thing about it was the sleeves—there was only one! Gaping, Artie asked as Kurt sat down at the kitchen table, "What happened to your jacket?"

"What, the sleeve?" Kurt took off the jacket and wiggled his hand through the empty hole where the sleeve should be. "I was messing around by the railroad tracks."

Artie stared at the empty hole.

"I jumped a freight. It was switching to drop off cars at the tile factory," Kurt went on, his eyes wide and earnest.

Over the train? Confused, Artie echoed, "You *jumped*?"

"Yeah, you know, I jumped a ride. The thing is, I jumped off without checking the main track, and an Amtrak came by and nearly pulled me under!"

Run down by a train! Artie blinked.

Just then Cozy swung into the kitchen, saying to Kurt, "You're pathetic."

"It's the truth, Cozy. You should have been there." Kurt gave her a broad smile. "I slipped out of my jacket; that's the only thing that saved me. That train sucked it down on the rail and cut the sleeve clean off."

Artie saw Kurt wink secretly in Cozy's direction. But Cozy was glaring. "Don't believe a word he says, Artie. He's the world's biggest liar."

Kurt winked again, this time in Artie's direction. "Your sister loves me," he whispered.

Cozy flounced out. Kurt laughed and picked up the plank of wood. "You're still sanding this?"

Artie nodded.

"It's good enough. Get the rest of the boards and the hammer and we'll hammer them together."

"Stay out of Dad's toolbox," Cozy yelled from the next room.

The noise was flowing in Artie's head again. Why was Cozy mad? It made it hard to enjoy his sanding. He didn't like anger.

Kurt wandered around the kitchen, quietly opening cupboard doors and looking under the sink. He asked in a low voice, "Where does your dad keep his tools?"

Artie thought a minute, then realized he didn't know. His ears burned, for it was something he should know, he was sure. But Cozy had already saved him. "Cozy said we couldn't," he reminded Kurt.

Kurt's eyes narrowed. "You don't have to do everything she says, you know. You never used to. You don't have to do anything *anyone* says, if you don't want to."

It was a new thought to Artie. It made his ears tingle and flooded his thinking space. He pushed at the sawdust with his fingers, making a small pile. "They tell me, Set the table. Find my shoes. Lift the rim. Don't cram my food." He rubbed the sawdust between his thumb and forefinger. There was a hurtful word down in his throat. He held it back and said, "I can't go out alone."

"Why not?" Kurt asked.

The word wouldn't stay down. He made a big letter *R* in the sawdust. "Because."

"Because why?" Kurt persisted.

"They think I'm retarded." It came out in a whisper, but it made a wind in his mind. Searching his friend's face, he added, "Because I forget. I'm not, though. I never have been. I'm not!"

"Of course you're not," Kurt said.

Encouraged by his smile, Artie whispered, "I want to go out. By myself, I mean. I think about it sometimes."

"I'd go with you," Kurt said.

Artie thought that over, then shook his head. "I mean alone. By myself."

With a shrug, Kurt flung himself out of the chair. "Do what you want, then. That's what I do."

Chapter 28

Cozy let the door go and smiled as Star pushed away a boy who had accidentally-on-purpose bumped her coming out of school. "Turn on your landing lights, Bryce. You're off the runway."

The boy blew her a kiss.

"Anyone I should know?" Cozy asked.

"Bryce Something-or-the-other. A sophomore, I think."

Grinning, Cozy slipped out of her jacket. It was a beautiful day. A fresh, sunny breeze, spring flowers blooming. And Micah had waited for her after English.

Star fumbled through the loose folds of her fabric belt for a roll of Lifesavers. "I'm starved. Let's get some hamburgers."

Over burgers and shakes, Cozy resisted the temptation to invite Star home, held back by the suspicion that for some reason she just didn't want to come. Some of her excuses recently had been pretty lame. She stirred her shake with her straw and listened as Star rattled off the list of prom queen candidates. "Who do you think will get it?" Star asked.

"It doesn't matter. If you don't go, you don't vote."

Star's eyes darkened. "You know, Coze, it's not too late. You could still ask someone."

"Be serious!"

"I am serious. Ask Micah Daniels."

Cozy ducked her head.

Star crowed. " 'Fess up. He likes you, doesn't he?"

Cozy protested, "I don't know. Who told you about Micah, anyway?"

"Why, is it a deep, dark secret? You couldn't tell me?"

"No, it's no secret. We're just *friends*." Cozy emphasized the word.

Star's mouth twitched. "So are you going to ask him to the prom? Friend to friend?"

"No way! You'll have to enjoy it without me."

Turning serious, Star said, "Why don't you call your mom and see if she'd let you off the hook this afternoon? You could come to my house for a change."

Cozy glanced at her quickly. Was that it? Star was tired of helping her with Artie? Struggling with conflicting emotions, Cozy folded and refolded her burger paper until it was the size of a postage stamp. "Mom's counting on me," she said at last.

"I'll tell you what, then. Come shopping with me tomorrow and help pick out my prom dress."

Star's voice was pleading. Anxious to keep things the way they'd always been, Cozy agreed to go shopping.

They were on their way out of the restaurant when Artie's old friend Biff hailed them from half a block away. He bummed a dollar off Star for a burger, then grinned at Cozy, and asked, "How about you? Any spare change?"

"Go on, give the boy a quarter, and maybe he'll leave us alone," Star teased.

Cozy gave him what was left of her change. He thanked her and tipped his hat with mock politeness.

"Show her what's under the hat. Go on, Biff, I dare you!" Star snatched the derby off his head to reveal a shaved head.

He tossed Cozy a quick glance. "What do you think?"

"Radical," Star said.

"I was asking Cozy."

"Whatever trips your trigger, Biff."

"Trip, trip." Star made a face at him and grabbed his hat.

"You're both jealous, that's all." Biff yanked back his hat and pulled it down hard on Star's head, leaving nothing but nose, mouth, and chin showing. He nudged Cozy. "Big improvement, huh."

Star flung off his hat and crossed her eyes. Biff sighed. "I give up. You don't know a cool dude when you see one."

"I'll let you know if I see one." Star ducked out of his reach, still laughing.

"That'll cost you a mint. A whole roll." Biff dived a hand into her pocketbook and snatched her Lifesavers.

Just like old times. Cozy tried to get into the spirit of it. But Artie kept getting in the way. The old Artie. Perhaps her expression gave her away, for Biff started into the restaurant then called back, "Hey, Coze! Tell Artie hi for me."

"Okay."

"I've been meaning to stop by," he said, shuffling from foot to foot.

"Any time," Cozy said.

A mischievous glint in his eye, Biff added, "Maybe while I'm there, he can teach me how to get away with it."

"Get away with it?" Cozy asked, uncomprehending.

He paused and shot Star a wicked grin. "Giving Star the old—"

"Shut up, Biff!" Star's voice cracked in alarm.

Cozy stared at them. "What's with you two?"

Biff tugged at the brim of his hat. "Nothing. Never mind," he mumbled, avoiding her gaze. "I gotta get something to eat. Tell Artie I'll drop by one of these days."

Beside her, Star dug nervously through her pocketbook for another roll of Lifesavers.

"Get away with what? Giving you *what?* What did he mean, Star?" Cozy persisted.

"I think it's the haircut. They clipped too deep."

"Star. You're covering up. I know you too well."

The lines on Star's face were strained, and she was flushing. Forcing a smile, she tried for her usual brightness, and still looked . . . guilty. But of what? Star's fingers were unsteady as she peeled down the paper and thrust the roll of Lifesavers in Cozy's direction.

"Emergency supplies. Here, have one."

Cozy took one, still waiting. "What was he talking about?"

"Why are you asking me? What am I, a mind reader?"

The candy in Cozy's mouth was suddenly too sweet. She jutted out her chin. "Don't give me that, Star. What is it you aren't telling me? What did Biff mean?"

"Biff shouldn't have said anything. I don't want to hurt you, Coze." Star's eyes misted. She blinked them clear, insisting, "It's no big deal, really. I wish Biff hadn't said anything."

"Just tell me!"

"All right, all right! But don't get mad at me!" In a rush, Star said, "It's Artie. The last time I was at your house, he put his hand on me. On my breast. But it's over and done."

He couldn't have, Cozy thought, but then came the sickening realization that it must be true—Star wasn't a liar.

Tears flooded her eyes. Star touched her arm, saying

softly, "Don't cry, Cozy. It's not such a big deal. He didn't stop to think, that's all. And when I yelled at him, he cried and said he was sorry. I handled it. See how you're taking it? See why I didn't want to tell you? Coze, come back here! Aw, Coze, why'd you make me tell you?"

Chapter 29

"What was Star wearing? Spandex, I suppose." Her mother's words dropped like rocks.

"Mom! It was Artie, Artie was the one—"

"I know, I know. But his hormones have kicked in, and there he is, nearly void of inhibitions. It *isn't* Star's fault. She's trying to be kind—I know that. But those sisterly hugs of hers . . . He's not a little kid, you know."

"No wonder she hasn't wanted to come over!" Cozy's eyes blurred.

"It's not fair, I know," said her mother more gently. She rubbed her eyes and murmured, "I'm sorry, Coze. This isn't fair to you—none of it's fair. But what can we do?"

Her concern prompted more tears. Cozy dabbed at them with a tissue and sniffed. "So what *are* we going to do?"

"I don't know yet. I never thought of something like this happening." Her mother picked up her knife and resumed chopping cabbage mechanically. "But it has to be dealt with, or how can Artie ever be independent?"

Cozy said nothing. Her mother was the strong one, the problem solver.

"Right now," her mother continued, "people may take into consideration what has happened to him, and make allowances. But that will change. In time they won't remember his circumstances, and then there will be no attempt to understand." She gazed at the shreds of cabbage, then put down the knife and went to the phone. "What's Star's number, Coze?"

"You're going to call her?" Cozy's face burned.

"I have to, don't you see? I have to know exactly what happened. Artie's doctors need to know—his therapists, too. We can't turn our heads, Cozette."

Her mother was right, of course. But Cozy'd had enough for one day. She left the room as her mother dialed the phone.

Later that evening, her mother's friend Natalie called and asked if she'd be free to baby-sit for Millie tomorrow. Relieved to have an excuse, Cozy called Star the next morning to say she couldn't go shopping.

"Maybe another time, then," said Star.

"Okay, sure."

"Coze? I'm sorry about what happened," Star said in a rush.

"Me, too."

The rest of the conversation was tense and too polite, and when it was over, Cozy was afraid things wouldn't ever be the same as they had been between them.

Chapter 30

Artie was glad it was his mother working at the computer. He was tired of the thing. It was like therapy—awful! And he hated it. But it was all right to watch. No one asked anything of him when he watched.

His mother was surrounded by books and note cards and pieces of paper. She tap-tap-tapped at the keys. His eyes were drawn to the calendar, but he did not know the day.

Across the room, his father was asleep in his chair. The television was on, with no one to watch it. Artie looked around for Cozy. Had she gone out? He walked from room to room, then sat down on the sofa again and tried to think where she had gone. Should he know? Or had no one told him?

"Mom?" he asked finally. Her fingers tapped the keys with a sudden burst of speed. "Mom?"

"Just a second, I want to get this down," she said without taking her eyes from the screen.

She *could* be at school. He glanced at the calendar again. Maybe that's where she was, at school.

"Mom?"

"Hmm?"

He hesitated, wondering if he should ask.

"What is it, Artie?"

He had his mother's attention now. But her fingers were poised over the keys. She was in a hurry.

"Are you going someplace?"

"No, why?"

"I just wondered, that's all. I just wondered." He stared at his shoes a minute, then lifted his head again. "Mom?"

"Hmm?"

"Is Cozy at school?"

"It's Saturday, Artie. She's baby-sitting for Millie Harper."

"Oh." He looked at the calendar, at the Saturday squares. Which one? he wondered. But she was typing again. So he went to the kitchen and stared out the window.

There was a boy in the alley below. He was throwing a rock. As Artie watched the boy draw his arm back, something moved in his mind. His pulse quickened. He pressed his nose to the screen and caught his breath. It was Kurt Parks. Kurt Parks! With the black hair and watery eyes and the smile that kept on smiling. Not just Kurt Parks who'd come to see him, but the old Kurt Parks. Two-in-one! It came together in his mind that they had always been one. He just hadn't pieced it together.

It excited him, the scroll in his head unrolling, revealing a picture. A picture of him and Kurt building. They had built a bicycle ramp, in that alley down there. They'd spent one whole summer jumping their bikes. More and more came, large chunks he'd been missing, chunks of Kurt and the things they had done.

It wasn't like the stories his mother told him, that she

said happened to him before his accident. He couldn't remember those. Just like the accident—he couldn't remember that accident. When her words painted pictures in his head, the pictures were of someone else. Even though she told him the stories were about him, he could not make the pictures be him.

But this time, the pictures were of him. Of him and Kurt Parks. Kurt had a yellow bike, but his was all chrome. It was a fast, beautiful dirt bike.

He could feel the wind in his face, just thinking about jumping that bike. Faster and faster he'd pedal. He'd hit the ramp full speed, pull up on the handlebars, and fly through the air for yards and yards. Then he'd touch ground and turn sharply to the right so his wheels would throw rocks and dust against the building. And when the air cleared, Kurt Parks was looking, smiling all over his face. Smiling a boastful smile, as if he could jump like that, too.

Kurt Parks. It dropped into his mind in reverse—*Skrap Truk*. Skrap Truk, clown words. He threw back his head and laughed. It felt so good. He laughed again and wanted to ask Kurt Parks if he still had his yellow bicycle. Tell him that he remembered about the bikes. And the ramp. And one Halloween when they'd soaped Mrs. Harding's window . . .

His mother's fingers were moving fast across the keys. His father was still sleeping. He hesitated, but no one said he couldn't go. So he opened the door and went out.

At the elevator a woman and her dog stepped out. It was a poodle dog. Mrs. Harding! He said, "Hi, dog," and stooped over to pat its curly head. But Mrs. Harding's big gnarled hand pulled hard on the leash, and the barking dog was jerked past him and down the corridor.

He stepped on the elevator, and the doors closed behind him. But the elevator didn't move. He stood with his back to the wall, waiting. And waiting. Why didn't it move? Was it broken? Had he broken it somehow? It made him anxious, not knowing. His shirt grew damp against his skin, and his pulse started to pound. Maybe he should get off. But how? How could he when the door was closed? As he stood wondering what to do, the elevator finally began to move.

When the door opened again, a man stepped on and looked at him in surprise. "Artie? What're you doing down here alone?"

It was a man he should know. But the name wouldn't come. And the man was waiting for an answer.

"Do your folks know you're down here?" the man asked.

Artie stepped out of the elevator, but the man dropped a hand on his arm. "Wait a second, Artie. I think we'd better check in with your folks."

The man talked to him, but Artie couldn't concentrate on his words. A big cloud was building inside of him. It was dark and gloomy. Maybe he didn't know this man. Maybe this man was a stranger. Maybe he shouldn't be riding the elevator with him. Don't talk to strangers. His mother had always told him, "Don't talk to strangers."

With his head full of clamoring thoughts, Artie was relieved when the elevator doors opened again and his mother was standing there. But her eyes were wide and scared.

"Artie! Thank God! Walter," she called down the corridor, "here he is. Chub found him."

Artie frowned. "I wasn't lost," he said.

But his mother was blinking fast and thanking the man. And his father came and thanked the man, too. Then he took Artie by the arm and led him into their apartment, saying in a tight, stern voice, "Artie, don't you ever do that again!"

"No, Artie, you can't. You simply can't," his mother chimed in. "You frightened us half to death!"

His head hurt and his stomach was full of sharp heavy stones. He did not like to see tears standing in his mother's eyes. Or the taut, deep lines on his father's face. His father was angry. Angry with him. His throat closed up, choked by salty tears, but the laughter came first. Then the tears, hot and wet on his face. Crazy laughter, hot tears. Crazy. Crazy boy.

"I don't want to be crazy," he said through laughing sobs. "I don't want to be crazy. I'd rather be dead than crazy."

His mother's arms were around him. "Artie, you're not crazy—you're not!" she insisted, her voice breaking. "Tell him, Walter. Explain it to him." She turned, including his father.

Through his tears, Artie saw his father's face, and heard him say in a deep gruff voice, "Don't be silly, Artie. Of course you're not."

Artie's mother patted his back and rocked him in her arms until the laughing sobs stopped. She told him in a choked voice that he wasn't crazy, that he'd had an accident and that slowly things were going to be better. But he had to be patient and work very hard. And she had to be patient, too. They all did.

And then finally, when his tears had stopped, she let go of him. She looked hard at his father, turned off the computer, piled up her books and papers, and said, "I'm ready now, Artie, if you'd like to go out."

"You go on with what you're doing, Brooke. I'll take him," his father said.

"As if I could concentrate now."

His father began buttoning his shirt. "Come on, Artie. I'll buy you a soda."

His mother's hands clenched into knots. Her eyes were dry now, but they were not happy. And her voice was not happy either. It reminded Artie of a TV commercial that showed inflamed muscles, red and wavy with pain. "Forget it, Walter. Go on and watch your game. I'll take him myself."

It was a fight. He hated fights and he had caused it. Artie caught his bottom lip between his teeth. He held out his hand, saying, "You, too, Dad. You come, too."

Chapter 31

"It isn't too late to get tickets for the game tomorrow, Walt. Why don't you give Chub a call and see if he'd like to go with you and Artie?"

Through her open door, Cozy heard more than she wanted to. The TV was blaring, her father was at the computer working on insurance forms, and her mother was working on her father. It had been almost a week since Artie had nearly gotten away from them. She was a little unclear about what had happened, exactly, but it had changed something between her parents.

"I could call about the tickets," her mother offered.

Cozy's father pushed the print button, and the printer whirred into action, but her mother talked above it.

"At least give it some thought, Walter. It'd be good for Artie, and I'm sure you and Chub would have a nice time."

Cozy heard her father rummaging in his briefcase. "Any envelopes around here?" he asked.

She kicked a stuffed elephant out of her way and picked up a pair of socks that had fallen behind the bed.

"The top desk drawer. So what do you say? Shall I call about the tickets?"

"If you want to go to the game, call about the tickets. I don't plan to go."

Cozy caught the door with her foot and gave it a shove. She remembered feeling left out when her father and Artie set off for Wrigley Field. Whether the Cubs won or lost, those two had always come home excited, talking about plays and pitches. A couple of times, she'd climbed on the El with them for the trip out to the ballpark and had still wound up feeling left out. There had been something special about her father and Artie sharing each other's enjoyment. Perhaps if her mother had ever gone with them, she would realize why her father was so reluctant to take Artie now.

With nothing more pressing to do, Cozy set about rearranging the furniture in her room. The only possibility for the bed was to put it so close to the closet that the door would only open partway. As she pushed and shoved, wedging it into position, her mother stepped in and looked around. "Would you like to have a break and take Artie for ice cream? I'll treat."

She was getting them out of the way. It must mean she was going to press the baseball issue. If they were going to argue, Cozy didn't want to hear it, anyway. "Okay. As soon as I finish here."

Her mother started to leave, then turned back. "Your bed's a little close to the closet door, isn't it?"

"I had to get it away from Artie's wall. He kicks the wall at night till I think I'll go nuts."

Her mother's face softened. "He's beginning to recognize his losses, Coze. It frustrates him."

"Me, too," she said, too softly for her mother to hear. Even then, she felt disloyal.

Sighing, Cozy combed her hair and tucked some change

into her pocket. Leaving the room as it was, she went to get Artie.

It had been raining, and the pavement was wet. But as Artie walked along with Cozy, the sun broke through the clouds. The air smelled fresh and clean. He wanted to breathe deeply, go slowly. But Cozy was walking fast. "Slow down. Wait for me."

Cozy turned and looked back, murmuring, "Sorry."

He looked around him, enjoying the green lawns. There were flowers and bushes and tall trees with thick limbs. And rain puddles on the sidewalk. Artie didn't know where they were, or where they were going. He started to ask, then didn't, afraid it was something he should know.

He stopped to watch some children. They were playing in rain puddles at the end of a driveway. Their feet were bare, their brown legs, too. Their voices made him smile.

He joined them, scuffing his shoes through a puddle.

"Take off your shoes. They'll get dirty," said the smallest of the children.

"I like dirty shoes," Artie said.

The little girl grinned up at him, commanding, "Watch me jump." Her knees jerked up, and her braids flew up, too, but her feet hardly left the ground. Artie threw back his head and laughed.

"Artie? Come on."

Artie glanced ahead to where Cozy was waiting. She had an anxious look on her face. Three boys walked past her, coming his way.

He jumped, too, and laughed at his wet shoes. The little girl laughed. So did the three boys. But their laughter was different.

"Geez," said one, "what a retard."

They laughed again as they brushed past him.

Artie curled his fists and stared after them.

"Let's go," said Cozy, turning him around. Artie didn't resist. He wanted to get away from the boys, from their laughter, from that word that he hated.

But there were other feelings, too, whirling around inside of him. And a sadness, like long empty corridors and cold white tombstones.

Chapter 32

A few days later, when Cozy came home, Artie opened his hand. He had written on his palm the letter *B*, so he wouldn't have to ask anyone where Cozy had gone.

"You were baby-sitting," he told her.

She smiled and said, "That's right. Very good, Artie."

He smiled, too, until his mother spoiled his mood by saying it was time to set the table.

"I'll do it," said Cozy.

But his mother shook her head. "It's Artie's job."

He didn't like the job. Everyone knew he didn't like it. He wanted to ask if he could have a different job, but his mother seemed to have forgotten him.

"How did the baby-sitting go today, Coze?" she asked Cozy.

"Pretty good. Millie and I played the fly game. I swatted—she counted. We broke all previous records." Cozy rubbed her hands under the faucet.

Their mother broke some spaghetti into a pot of boiling water. She glanced his way and said, "Artie, dear, you'd better get started."

Cozy did not offer to do it again. Artie sighed and got a plate from the cupboard. His father's plate. He put it on the table. He picked out a fork and put it beside the plate, then returned for a knife and finally a spoon. There. One place was set, and he had not asked a single question! He glanced up to see if anyone noticed how well he had done. His mother was buttering bread. Cozy was talking, telling his mother things, gesturing and smiling, but not at him. They had both forgotten him.

His father came home with a box. It was a white box with red stripes and a very good smell. "Hi, Dad. I set your place first, see?" he said, pointing.

"So you did. Thanks, Artie."

His shoulder warmed where his father's hand had clasped it. But the anxious, left-out feeling remained. He sniffed the good smell and asked, "What's in the box? Is it chicken? It smells like chicken."

"The Colonel's best," said his father, smiling. He offered the box with a kiss to Artie's mother.

"Chicken?" She brushed her eyelid where the kiss had landed.

"I thought I'd surprise you. What with your deadline, you haven't had much time for cooking."

"I appreciate the gesture, but where were you last night when Cozy was putting together this spaghetti sauce?"

"Yes, Dad, where were you?" Cozy chimed in, kiddingly.

Artie wanted them to eat. It was such a good smell. His nostrils flared, taking it in. He rubbed his stomach. "I'm hungry—let's eat."

"We're all hungry, Artie. Please finish setting the table. Cozy's spaghetti is almost ready."

"If it's all the same to everyone, I'd prefer chicken," said his dad.

"What, and miss Cozy's spaghetti? She gave it her best effort."

"Chopping onions and burning my eyes. What a job!" Cozy wiped her brow and grinned.

But not at me, Artie thought. None of them seemed to see him. He was like an extra fork on the table. A fork no one needed. Was it such a big thing, that Cozy had made spaghetti? He tilted his head and pulled at his ear.

"Artie, we're waiting for you to finish the table," his mother said, and the tone of her voice made the cloud inside grow. He looked at Cozy, at his father. Their faces said the same thing. "Hurry up, Artie. We're waiting, we're always waiting for you. Hurry, hurry, hurry."

He looked and he looked at the screen in his head and he knew they had not looked at the other boy that way. He could not get it right in his head, why that boy had gone away.

"Accident," they said. "Head injuries." But all the while their eyes said, "Retarded." He looked at his hands and saw them tremble. He felt the trembling inside, too, where his muscles and bones were—tremble and tremble until he thought they would fly apart.

"Artie, please! Do it now," said his mother.

Her voice stung his ears, clear and sharp and hurting. The cloud burst wide open and out of it spilled, not tears but the hateful high laughter. He tried to choke it back, heard his own voice shrill, "I'm not setting the table. It's a baby job. I won't do it!"

They were silent, eyes round, mouths hanging open. Hot, salty tears slid down his cheeks, and still the hateful laughter would not be still.

His mother spoke more softly, saying, "Artie, honey, it

isn't funny. Think, now. What do you feel? You're upset, aren't you?"

"Upset." He nodded and nodded, wanting her to grab him, and grab the shadow boy, too. Join them together and make it right again.

"You didn't mean to laugh, did you?"

No, no! Hateful stupid laughter, shouldn't come. It wasn't funny.

"All right, then," she said, as if it were settled.

"I'll help you, Artie," said Cozy, giving him a plate.

The plate was cool and smooth between his hot fingers, but it could not calm the storm inside him. Suddenly he lifted his arms high over his head and flung the plate down, cursing and cursing until there was no other sound in the room but his cursing. And for a moment he felt power—a clean, pure surge of it making him tall and bold and unfailing.

But his father leaped toward him, caught his arm with rough fingers, and yelled angrily, "Shut up, Artie. Now!"

He shrank and shrank, until he had no more substance than his sobs. "I don't want to do it, I don't!"

"We all have to do things we don't want to do. Some mornings, I don't want to go to work. Some nights I don't want to come home. But I do, don't I? *Don't I?*"

"Walt, please!" wailed his mother.

They stood for a moment, frozen. Then his father let go of Artie's arm. His shoulders sagged, and he rubbed his face with both hands, his fingers sliding beneath his glasses.

"Coze, would you get the broom, please?" said his mother.

"No," said his father, his hands coming down. "Artie made the mess. Artie's going to clean it up."

The sorrow rolled up out of Artie's belly and made his

throat raw and swollen. But he got the broom and tried to sweep. Cozy moved toward him and would have helped, but his father stood in her way.

"That's good enough," he said finally. "Now finish setting the table like your mother told you."

"Cozy, get a platter for the chicken," said his mother.

But his father picked up his briefcase and walked out of the kitchen. "Nothing for me, thanks. I'm not hungry."

Chapter 33

Later Artie followed Cozy to her room and sat on the edge of her bed, watching her snatch clothes from her closet and toss them down on the bed.

He dropped his hands between his knees and looked down at his shoes. They had deep creases in the toes. But there were no strings. There should be strings. He bounced his heels up and down.

Cozy turned, looking at him. Her brows came together, and her mouth turned down. "Would you quit that, Artie?"

He looked at his hands. They were empty. And he had not spoken. At least, his mouth didn't feel as if it had spoken. "Quit what?" he asked.

"Bouncing. You're making the bed squeak."

"Oh." He gave another bounce. Yes, it did squeak. He hadn't noticed before. It wasn't a bad squeak, though. It was a squeak with a regular rhythm. Regular rhythms were okay. It was the irregular ones that kept you listening for the final beat. Those were the grating sounds. They kept a person on edge, listening. He bounced his heels again, a regular two-count: *It-tee, it-tee, it-tee, it-tee, it-tee . . .*

"Artie, stop it or get out!"

"I'll stop," he said quickly.

"What're you doing in here, anyway? I want to change my clothes."

Artie thought a moment. He remembered his father so silent in the living room, and the storm in the kitchen. He had caused it. "Dad's mad," he said.

Cozy responded with a flip of her head. "It was a stupid fight, Artie. Just forget it, okay?"

Their mother came in with a stack of laundry. She sat down on the bed beside him and patted his knee.

Cozy tugged at a pair of jeans, knocking over the pile.

His mother straightened it. "Are you going somewhere?"

"Out."

Artie watched as Cozy whisked a pair of peach-colored socks out of the middle. He saw his mother straighten the pile a second time.

"Out where?"

"Anywhere away from here."

Cozy's voice was like broken glass. Artie didn't like it that way. "I can go with you, Cozy. Where shall we go?"

"You've got spaghetti on your face. Why don't you go wash it?"

It wasn't her words, but rather the way she looked at him. He saw his mother frown, an unspoken warning directed at Cozy. It made him feel even smaller. So he got to his feet and shuffled out the door without looking back.

Chapter 34

In her hurry to put home behind her, Cozy didn't notice the motorcycle until it screeched to a stop on the sidewalk right in front of her. Her alarm faded quickly as she recognized the rider. It was Micah Daniels.

"Going my way?" He grinned.

She touched the handlebars. "Is this yours?"

"It belongs to a friend of mine who swapped with my brother for the evening. He had a date for the prom and needed a car. I figured you'd be there."

"At the prom?" Cozy shook her head.

"How come?"

Blushing, she nudged the front wheel of the cycle with her foot. "You'd better get that thing off the sidewalk before a cop comes along."

He shot her a daring glance. "Nobody asked you either, huh?"

"What do you mean, 'either'? You didn't have to wait to be asked."

"Neither did you. You could have asked me and I would have said yes." Micah's eyes twinkled, and it was impossible not to grin back.

"Really?" Cozy asked.

"It's not too late, you know. We could still go."

"I don't think so."

"Why not?" He patted the space on the seat behind him. "Let's check it out."

"Like this?"

"I'm game if you are."

Cozy tapped her foot, considering the idea.

"If you're waiting for a pumpkin coach and eight shining steeds . . ."

Cozy laughed. Suddenly shy about looking him in the eye, she checked out the bike. "I told my mom I was going to the Dairy Queen."

With a long-suffering sigh, Micah leaned back and locked his arms across his chest. "So let's explore your options. One, you can go to the prom. Two, you can live recklessly and have a triple-scoop hot-fudge banana split."

"Oh, shut up." And laughing, she threw caution aside and swung a leg over the seat.

Micah passed back his helmet. "In lieu of flowers . . . Hang on."

Cozy snapped down the face shield as Micah kick started the bike. She politely laid one hand on either side of his waist. But as they lurched off the curb and roared into the street, self-preservation took over, and she grabbed on tight.

The rushing traffic, the rumble of the motor, the color and sound and motion all blended together in a giant rush. Micah leaned into a sudden left turn. Cozy took a sharp breath, certain the bike was going to skid onto its side. She stiffened and leaned hard to the right. Amazingly, the bike righted itself. They kept humming along.

Micah called over his shoulder, "You've got to lean with the turns, left on a left turn and right on a right turn."

Theoretically, it seemed wrong. But she took his word for it, nodded, and braced herself for the next turn. It went against every fiber of her being to lean toward the pavement that seemed to be rising up to meet them, but she gritted her teeth and forced herself to do it.

"Take it easy. You're getting the hang of it," Micah called back, which she interpreted to mean he'd appreciate it if she'd take her fingernails out of his stomach.

Micah turned down a less busy street, and gradually Cozy's fears subsided. She began to enjoy the feel of the bike beneath her, the breeze whipping at her clothes, the freedom of movement.

The scent of Right Guard floated back, and Cozy smiled, remembering how Artie used to hurry home from a baseball game, change his clothes, and spray Right Guard on his shirt, so their mother would think he'd taken a shower.

By the time they slowed for Willow Park, Cozy had noticed other things: the confidence with which Micah handled the bike, the way his hair curled over the neck of his T-shirt, the tautness of his muscles beneath her hands. His closeness gave her another kind of rush.

The prom was being held at the south end of the park, at the pavilion, which overlooked a small lake where ducks and pedal boats skimmed along beneath the setting sun. It was a balmy evening. The couples on the balcony around the pavilion, dressed in formal gowns and tuxes, bore little resemblance to the jeans-clad hordes that crowded the halls at school.

Micah veered off the street and parked beneath a willow at the lake's edge. He climbed off the bike and opened her face mask. "So what do you think?"

She smiled back at him. "So far so good."

"Want to walk along the lake?"
"Okay, but I have to be home by dark."
"Before you lose your glass slipper?"
She grinned. "Right."

Chapter 35

Artie strained forward on the sofa as the door closed behind Cozy. Where was she going? Had he been told, and he'd forgotten? It was on his tongue to ask, but his father was watching TV. He did not look in Artie's direction, so Artie held his question and looked at the TV, too.

It was just men in dark suits talking and talking. Dull colors, no bright music. He saw the remote on the arm of his father's chair and thought about finding a better channel. But the lines in his father's face were deep and long, and he was afraid to ask if he could.

The muscles in Artie's legs twitched as he thought about Cozy going out. He wanted to go out, too. Just like Cozy had done. He thought it and thought it and finally got up and started for the door. But when he looked back, his father's face was turned his way. Artie's pulse quickened, and a warning rang in his head. So he veered off toward the closet instead.

His old shoes were there, the too small shoes with the raveled laces and the scuffs and creases. He carried them back to the sofa and sat down, just as his mother came into the living room. Holding his good old shoes, he wanted to ask if he could, just this once, go out. But she stopped behind his father's chair and stood there for so long that he forgot what it was he wanted to ask.

His mother put a hand on his father's shoulder. His father kept looking at the TV, but by and by, he lifted a hand and covered hers.

"Why don't you come into the kitchen, and I'll heat up that chicken?" she said.

His father didn't answer. But in a moment, he got up and followed her into the kitchen, and he didn't invite Artie to come along. Forgotten, Artie thought. Forgotten again. He looked at the remote, but it held no appeal.

His head was full of thoughts waiting for him to call them up:

Lonely thoughts.

Angry thoughts.

Hurtful thoughts.

Daring thoughts.

He was least afraid of the daring thoughts. Looking back across the room over his shoulder, he saw the kitchen door firmly closed.

Once he was on his feet, it was easy. He took his good old shoes and closed the door softly. Ahead of him, the elevator doors swung open for Mrs. Harding and her dog. He hurried to catch up. She was a tall woman with a large wrinkled face, squiggly red lines on her nose, and hair that stood out from her head like bent wires. She looked his way, and for a split second Artie saw alarm in her eyes.

Why? Artie checked himself over, then looked back at her. She stiffened her loose chin and said, "One."

He looked at her questioningly.

"One," she said again with a fluttery wave of her blue-veined hand. "Push one."

His head rushed with sound. The buttons! He dropped

a shoe in his hurry to make up for his mistake. But when his fingers finally reached the button panel, her hand had brushed past him.

"Never mind—I'll do it myself," she said, and the elevator began to move.

Artie bent down to pick up his shoe. The dog yapped at him. It was a curly dog, short-legged, with saggy old eyes.

"Hush, now," said Mrs. Harding. The dog wagged its stump tail and kept barking.

Artie followed them off the elevator and out the front door. He might have kept following, but Mrs. Harding looked back over her shoulder, and again he saw her alarm.

He watched her nervous steps and saw a picture in his head. It was Halloween, and he had soaped her windows. He saw a picture of her grabbing him and making him wash them. He wondered that *he* wasn't afraid. He was sorry, though, sorry he'd soaped her windows. She was old and her dog was old and he wouldn't do it again. Maybe if she knew he wouldn't soap her windows, she wouldn't be afraid.

There were cars in the street with their windows down. He could hear their music. The air was warm. A barefoot girl was jumping rope on the sidewalk. He saw no light to cross by, so he turned down the alley. The yellow cat was there. He quickened his steps, calling, "Here, kitty, kitty, kitty." The cat turned and twitched its satin-smooth ears.

Artie crouched down beside the cat. Dropping his shoes, he pushed his hand across the soft fur. "You're a good old cat, you are. I'm building a house for you. Kurt and me, we're building a cat house. You'll like that, won't you?"

He slid down to the ground, feeling the sun-warmed brick wall against his back. The day was fading in the narrow strip of sky above him. It made long shadows on the bricks across from him, quiet shadows. It was quiet in his head, too, and his body felt loose and easy and free.

"Meow?" the cat asked.

He stretched out his hand. The cat brushed against him, then walked across his legs with soft paws. He tickled the cat under the chin, and it meowed again, arching its neck and slanting its eyes in a smiling wink. Artie felt the rich rumble in the cat's throat, the sandpaper roughness of its tongue. The cat rolled over on his lap, and he saw it was not a tomcat after all, but a mother cat with nursing kittens somewhere.

He stroked the cat until she grew restless. She wriggled free and moved away in little runs and pauses, as if she were leading the way. "Okay, cat, I'm coming," he said, struggling to his feet.

He followed the cat to the railroad tracks. He had to let his legs do all the work scrambling up the steep ditch so he wouldn't drop his shoes. Warm and panting, he sat down on a shiny rail to catch his breath. But the cat crossed over to the far ditch and disappeared into the grass. Hunting, Artie thought. She was a hunting cat. Independent and free. Looking for dinner. Cats needed to be alone to hunt. He did not try to follow.

The sun hung on the horizon over the tracks, casting a shimmering path and asking Artie to come see.

So he walked toward the sun, carrying his good old shoes. It wasn't easy walking. The rocks slipped beneath his feet when he moved along the outside of the rails. On the inside, the ties between the rocks were too close for easy strides. Back and forth he went, trying the inside, then the outside, stumbling, stopping, looking around.

Further down the tracks, lined up in front of the orange sun, were train cars—flatcars sitting silent and empty. Artie looked back over his shoulder. It was dull by comparison. No sunset colors, no train cars. It was not the way to go. Forward, that was the way.

"I'm going," he said to himself, measuring out his steps, hitting ties where he could.

It was a rumbling like distant thunder that stopped him. He dropped to his knees and put his hands to the rails, feeling them hum and shiver. Train coming! Which way? He shaded his eyes. Yes, it was coming toward him. It made his ears tingle to hear the sound grow. The train whistled, a hoarse whistle. A freight train, skimming down the rails toward him.

He looked ahead at the cars on the side rail. They were close enough to count the wooden pallets stacked on them. And the box factory! It was there, just as he knew it should be. Just as in past days when he'd run along and climbed on as the train slowed to switch to the side rail and pick up the loaded cars. His heart pounded and his palms were slick, gripping the leather of his old shoes. In his head, he saw pictures of himself running fast, of things he used to do. Long, swift, even strides: his hand gripping a narrow rung on the ladder; his body in motion, swinging up, onto the train until he had left the ground and the ladder trembled beneath his hands and feet. He felt the wind in his face, tickling his nose, blowing back his hair, burning his eyes.

He could do it. He *would* do it! He started to run, but something misfired. His body did not heed what was on the screen in his head, his feet did not move as he signaled them to, and the train was growing larger, closer. There was too little time.

Artie threw his shoes in the ditch and followed them down. He stood in waist-high weeds watching the train come. It shook the ground as it passed, boxcars swaying on the rails. It was a singing rhythm, a marching rhythm, *clackety-clack, clackety-clack*. A traveling rhythm.

It seemed, as he watched, that it went too fast to catch. *But not for that other boy*. That boy was fast. Hadn't he been trying and trying to catch him? But he was always a shadow—a dim ghostlike shadow hovering nearby, then flitting out of reach.

Chapter 36

As they made their way around the lake, the music from the pavilion drifted across the water. The sun cast a coral glaze on the tranquil water, and ducks bobbed for minnows along the edge. They stopped to watch them awhile. Cozy picked a leaf from a low-hanging maple and ripped it along the veins, saying, "It's nice here, isn't it?"

Micah smiled, then pushed his hands into his pockets and inclined his head toward the pavilion. "But the action's inside. Let's go get you a dance card."

Cozy laughed. "I don't think so."

"Why not?"

"Dressed like this?"

He caught her hand and pulled her toward the pavilion, teasing. "Just one dance. Come on—it'll be fun."

Beginning to be afraid he was serious, she protested, "I'd die of embarrassment. Really, I would."

"Chicken." But he smiled as he said it, and offered no objections when she turned back the way they'd come. Side by side, they retraced their steps around the lake to the motorcycle. Cozy put the helmet on and climbed on the back of the bike.

Three sidewalks broke up the pavilion's green lawn. One approached the center steps of the portico that fronted the pavilion. Another ran to a set of steps on the right, and a ramp led up to the portico on the left. Cozy took all this in at a glance as Micah shifted gears and made a slow pass in front of the pavilion.

Once past it, Micah turned the bike around, saying over his shoulder, "Last chance for a dance."

"I'll pass," Cozy called back.

A couple was just arriving, a thin girl in a white dress, who lifted her long skirts gracefully as she climbed the center steps, and her escort. Two guys in black tuxedos were on the ramp, drinking from long-stemmed glasses.

Micah made a leisurely circle through Willow Park, past dog walkers, Frisbee players, and kids on swings. They were almost to the columns that marked the entrance when Micah made a U-turn, saying over his shoulder, "You really should have a memento."

"That's okay."

"No, it's not okay. Hang on."

They drove back through the park toward the pavilion. Cozy tightened her grip as he picked up speed and approached the pavilion from the left. He shifted down, hit the sidewalk, shifted again, and headed straight for the ramp.

Cozy protested weakly, but all that came back on the wind was his laughter. Their rush up the ramp came so unexpectedly that the couples on the portico froze in place. How was he planning to get back down? Cozy worried. "Not the steps, Micah!"

He was going to do it anyway, she was sure. Cozy closed her eyes and buried her helmet-clad head against his back. At the last second, he screeched his brakes, dropped a foot to steady the bike as they pivoted, and headed back toward the ramp. Cozy opened her eyes in time to see a girl in a low-bodiced dress leap back and yelp, "Daniels, you're crazy!"

The boys on the ramp had recovered from their surprise. They laughed and raised their punch glasses in a salute. Micah snatched a glass in passing. The contents of it sloshed back in a trail down the leg of Cozy's jeans.

"Your keepsake," he said, passing her the glass.

Cozy closed her hand around the stem, then looped her arm around his waist again, the blood still rushing in her ears. Once out of the park, she glanced back over her shoulder. No sirens, no red lights, no one in hot pursuit.

Micah was laughing. She felt it through his shirt first, then heard it coming back on the breeze.

"She's right—you *are* crazy!" Cozy said, laughing as well.

Chapter 37

There wasn't much room on the flatcar. The pallets had been packed in tightly and close to the edge. Artie sat down and curled his legs beneath him. He held his shoes in his lap and listened in his head for the cheers, for the high-flying surge of pleasure. But it was quiet in his thinking space. There was nothing on the screen. Where was the victory in climbing on a flatcar when the flatcar was on the side track—unmoving?

Shoulders drooping, he gazed at the tall wire fence and the locked gates of the box factory. The place was silent and deserted, with no one to yell, "Get down from there, boy." No one to care what he did.

Off to the east, he could see the end of the train. It had slowed—but it was still moving. He heard creaking, like rusty hinges, then the bumping as the train stopped. He got to his feet, watching and listening. Was the train switching? Was that all the noise? Yes! "Come back here, train," he said, and he knew with a lifting of spirits that it would. It would come for the cars, link up, and take them away.

He clutched his shoes, his heart beating faster. He could

ride the train down the tracks, feeling the rumble beneath him, the evening wind in his face—faster and faster, until he caught that boy. It was a funny idea. A clown idea, for a shadow was not a thing you could catch. He laughed out loud and yet, even as he laughed, he made a desperate wish that it could be so.

His head was so full of his thoughts, he did not see Kurt until Kurt was almost upon him.

"Hey, Artie!" he called in his big smiling voice. "What're you doing?"

"Riding. I'm going to ride."

Kurt looked at him, his smile still there, but fading. He scratched his black hair, scrambling the straight white part. "Think you should?"

"I can," he said, a faint noise creeping into his head. "I've done it before."

"Lots of times," Kurt said. "But that was before."

The noise in his head whispered what it read on Kurt's face. "You think I can't do it."

"I didn't say that."

But Kurt's face was saying it. Over and over. Artie gripped his shoes tighter. "Aren't we friends?"

"Yeah, sure." Kurt turned his hands up and lifted his shoulders, and his smile came back, wide and careless. "Sure, we are. Scoot over. I'm coming up."

Artie scooted. They sat waiting as the train backed, lumbering side to side as it came. There were a number of cars in front of them, but the impact of the train connecting was still a hard, lurching jolt. For a moment there was no movement at all, and a worried hum filled Artie's head. "What's wrong?"

"Nothing's wrong. We'll go in a minute. Listen, Artie, once it gets going, you've got to be ready to jump. You remember how to do it, don't you?" Kurt swung onto the ladder, down to the first rung. He let go with one arm and one leg. "Like this. And you look to make sure there's nothing in the way of your landing."

Artie nodded, but his thoughts were drifting. The boy was there, on the screen in his head. Riding, riding until he was tired of riding—then jumping free. He would do as the shadow boy did.

The train creaked beneath him, beginning to roll. His heart leaped to his throat. Going! They were going! He pushed his shoes behind him, then reached back and gripped the bottom pallet, the thin lumber rough against his fingers.

They hadn't gone far, and they weren't moving fast yet. There was just a small wind in his face, but it lifted the damp hair from his forehead. Already Kurt was moving toward the ladder. He had his foot on the rung, and was grinning all over his face. "Follow me, Artie. Jump right after me, okay?"

Artie nodded, and Kurt swung out and jumped. He ran along beside the train, never losing his balance. "Okay, move to the ladder now. Come on, Artie, move!"

The wind was coming faster now. It flattened back Kurt's hair as he ran along, stretching a hand toward him.

"Come on, Artie! Jump!"

Kurt wasn't smiling anymore. There was a startled look in his eyes. He grabbed hold of the rung and swung up again. "You aren't scared, are you? Here, scoot down. Get on the ladder beside me. We'll jump together."

"I'm not jumping," said Artie, and once the words were out, he felt as if he had known all along that he wouldn't.

"Of course you're jumping," Kurt argued, not understanding. "Give me your hand. I'll help you."

Artie moved back, out of reach. He shook his head. "I'm riding, Kurt. I'm riding."

"Okay," said the boy. "But just a little further. And this time when I say *jump*, you have to jump."

No, he didn't have to. He didn't want to. He wanted to ride, to catch the boy he used to be—catch him and hang on until they were one. And if he couldn't catch him . . . if he couldn't do that, then he'd keep riding, to someplace where there was no one to tell him to set the table, find lost things, and hurry, hurry, hurry.

His eyes watered. The wind was stronger now, blowing his throat dry and whistling in his ears. Artie laughed out loud at the knowledge that he could do as he pleased.

But Kurt wasn't laughing. "We're picking up speed. We've got to jump now, right now while we still can," he shouted urgently over the *clackety clack* traveling song. He rushed toward Artie, clinging to the pallets with one hand. Grabbing him, he pulled Artie toward the ladder with the other hand.

"No! I'm not jumping—I'm riding. I'm riding—let go!" Artie yelled, but Kurt, stronger than he, was pulling and shouting, and not smiling at all.

Artie saw Kurt's foot, reaching for the ladder, wobble. Kurt clutched madly for balance, and suddenly Artie saw what he had not seen before. Careless, laughing devil-may-care Kurt was afraid!

Artie saw the fear in Kurt's face and realized that Kurt was afraid because of him. He stopped struggling, suddenly understanding what he was doing. Crazy! Freakin' crazy! He could not catch that boy. And he was scaring Kurt. Kurt was his friend, scared but trying. Trying to help, just like the others: his mother, his father, his sister, and Star.

Ashamed, he yelled, "I'll jump. I will, Kurt. I'll jump."

White-faced, Kurt screamed back, "Now! Right now, then. Right after me!"

Kurt let go. Artie saw him leap free, hit the rocks, then the ditch, and roll. Artie's heart pounded. Hurt? Was he hurt? No, Kurt was on his feet again, running after the train.

Artie edged one foot onto the ladder and looked over his shoulder at the rocks rushing past in a blur.

He slid his other foot onto the ladder.

Took a deep breath.

Let go, hands. Let go, feet.

Flying, flying.

Ground rushing up.

Dragging him down.

Fading, fading into darkness.

Floating, drifting. Silence.

Chapter 38

Cozy jumped off the back of the bike and rushed into the emergency room entrance. She looked frantically down the corridor and saw her mother coming out of the lounge.

"He's got a broken arm and a few cuts and bruises, but he's doing all right," she said.

All the horrors Cozy had imagined on the endless ride to the hospital gave way to tears. Her mother hugged her. "My note scared you, didn't it? I'm sorry. I was in such a hurry—I'm not even sure what I wrote."

Cozy wiped away her tears. "Kurt told me. He was waiting when I got home."

"How did you get here?"

"Micah brought me. Will they let me see Artie?"

"They've taken him up to the second floor. Room two-thirty-one. Your Dad's signing papers."

"They're keeping him?"

"Just for a day or two. There's too much swelling in the arm to set it tonight. Go on up, if you want to. We'll be along shortly."

* * *

Artie was awake, but groggy—they must have given him a painkiller. His arm was bandaged, his hands were scraped, and there was a stitched gash along his temple. Blood had dried in his hair.

He tried to sit up in bed, but winced and eased back down into the pillow. Cozy patted his good arm tearfully.

"Artie, you're too much! Jumping trains, no less. I could kill Kurt Parks."

Groggily, Artie murmured, "He took my shoes."

"Who, Kurt?"

"No, that other boy—he took them."

Artie was talking so softly she could scarcely hear him.

"Never mind. Just so you're all right. We can find your shoes tomorrow."

"He laughed when he took them," Artie said, his voice strained. "They were his shoes, and he wanted them. He tricked me."

This has to be the sedative, thought Cozy. "Let it go, Artie. It doesn't matter. You're going to be okay, and that's all that matters."

Finally his gaze focused and met hers. "I'm sorry, Cozy. I'm sorry."

"It's okay," she murmured.

"I wanted to catch him, but I couldn't. I'm sorry, I'm sorry."

"Catch who?"

"That boy. That shadow boy I used to be."

A nurse came to make certain Artie's arm was properly elevated. Cozy's parents followed her in. Her mother still looked shaken, her father tense and restless.

The nurse took Artie's temperature, then left. Cozy's

father stepped up to the bed. "How does your arm feel? Does it hurt much?"

Artie shook his head. His eyes looked small and lost.

Cozy's father touched a bruise on Artie's face. He turned Artie's good hand over, looked at the cuts and scratches made by the rocks, and closed his own strong fingers around it.

"Are you mad at me?" Artie whispered.

"No, just scared," said his father.

Tears blurred Cozy's vision as her mother reached for her father's hand. She took Cozy's hand, too, linking them all together.

After a moment, her father moved away from the bed and adjusted the curtains. He asked Artie again if his arm was hurting. He offered Artie water from the pitcher the nurse had left. Artie didn't answer. His eyes were drifting shut.

"Are you about ready to go?" Cozy's father asked them, when Artie seemed to be sleeping soundly.

Her mother shifted in the chair. "I don't want to leave him alone," she said. "He may need something."

Cozy's father looked at Artie for a long time, then helped her mother out of the chair, saying, "You and Cozy go on. I'll stay."

"Are you sure?" her mother asked softly.

He nodded. "He and I need some time together. It's been awhile since we had a good talk."

Chapter 39

Artie's mother came to the hospital early the next morning. She was there when the doctor put the cast on his arm. After breakfast his father showed him again how to use the remote control on the TV; then his parents went home. Cozy came in, right after lunch, with Star.

Artie beckoned for them to come closer. "Look, I can work this TV. And I can make this bed move, too, just by pushing a button. See?" He held the button, and the top portion of the bed came up, up, up, until he was sitting.

"Careful, you'll make a sandwich of yourself," Star warned. "An Artie sandwich—hold the mayo, please."

His head was still tender, and it throbbed when he laughed. Gingerly, his fingers touched near the wound. "I've got stitches. Did you know, Star?"

"Sixteen of them, Cozy told me. Which is what you deserve for playing on a train. You could have killed yourself. Don't you ever do that again!" Star scolded, but it was not a mean scolding. There was love in her voice, and in her eyes, too. When he turned the hurt side of his head toward her, she winced. "You've been butchered. What a haircut! I hope they didn't charge extra for that."

"It's just for the stitches, see?" he said, anxious for her to know he wasn't missing any hair on the other side of his head.

"It'll grow back," Cozy said, dropping a heavy white plastic bag into his lap.

"In the meantime, if you should need a transplant, I think we've got a close match here." Star caught the end of her long ponytail in her hand as if she were offering it to him.

Artie grinned back at her. He pulled at the package with one hand. "What is it, Cozy? A present? Is it a present?"

"Yes, it's a present. I spent every dime of my baby-sitting money, and Star had to kick in to make up the difference." She motioned with her hands. "Go on—open it."

There was a box inside the sack. A white box. He pulled it out and took off the lid. There was a splash of red-and-black leather. His mouth dropped open. "Shoes! Ankle shoes."

"They're high-tops, Artie. Do you like them?" Star asked.

He pulled one shoe out of the box, lifted it to his face, and breathed in, smelling the leather. He slid his hand over the black insets, the red laces. "I like them. They're beautiful."

Star and Cozy beamed back at him. "Try them on."

He pushed back the sheet, but it was hard to sit up with his arm in a cast. Cozy helped him, but even then, the motion made his head swim, and he had to wait a minute. By then, Cozy was on the floor in front of him, loosening the laces and fitting one shoe over his bare foot.

"If they aren't the right size, we can exchange them. There, step down," she said, steadying him as he got to his feet. "What do you think?"

Careful of his reeling head, he took a few steps and

looked down, wiggling his toes. The leather was stiff and snug against his foot. It felt like a new shoe—*his* new shoe. "I'll take them," he said.

"New shoes? Hey, wow!" called a voice from the door. Artie turned to see Kurt amble in, wearing his big quarter-moon smile. He had on a long black trench coat, and the pockets were wiggling.

"Are you cold?" Artie asked.

"No. I'm about to roast." Kurt fanned his perspiring face, peering out into the hallway. Then he closed the door.

Artie saw Cozy frowning. She opened her mouth, but before she could say anything, Artie said hurriedly, "These are my new shoes. Cozy got them for me. Cozy and Star."

Kurt slipped his hand into his coat pocket. "I brought you a present, too. Pick a color—yellow, yellow-striped, or buff."

Artie ran through the choices in his head. "Yellow," he said. Then his mouth dropped open as Kurt drew from his pocket a tiny yellow kitten. Artie held it in one hand, cradled against his body. Its tiny claws snagged his hospital gown. "Good kitty, good little kitty," he whispered softly.

"Where in the world did you get him?" Cozy asked.

"From the basement of my building. There's four of them. I've been playing with them and getting them tame." Kurt took kittens from his various pockets and passed them around. Watching Artie, he grinned and added, "Think you can teach it to sleep in the cat house we built?"

The house he had built! Artie hugged the kitten close, feeling its throat rumble. "You're mine—I'm going to keep you, yellow kitten." He turned toward the door as it opened. A nurse with a bored expression strolled in. "Get those cats out of here," she said, scarcely blinking. "The doctor's making his rounds. With any luck, he'll send you home."

Artie relinquished the kitten and put his tongue over the thermometer the nurse popped into his mouth. He watched Star and Kurt, shoulder to shoulder, squeeze out the door.

When they had gone, Cozy picked the lone shoe out of its box and loosened the laces. "Want to put on your other shoe?"

He nodded. His left foot looked bare next to his bright red right foot. She worked it onto his foot and said quietly, "That other boy, the one you were trying to catch yesterday? He wore white high-tops. I could still get you white ones, if you'd rather."

He bent his knee to pluck at the bright red laces. "I like these shoes—I like them a lot."

She nodded, smiling an unsteady smile. "I thought you would. I looked for your old shoes, the ones that other boy took. I walked up and down the tracks. But I couldn't find them."

It took the air from his lungs. How had she known? He didn't remember telling her about the shadow boy. He didn't think he'd told anyone. "He's gone," he said, plucking at the sheet.

"No, not completely." She tied the shoe snug and pushed at the toes with her fingers. "There's still some of that boy in you, Artie. We're lucky to have you."

Then it was all right? It didn't matter that the boy had gotten away? Anxiously, he searched her face. She grinned and said, "Scoot over. I want to try out this bed."

His head quivered when her shoulder bumped his, but he slid over and gave her the control.

"You're a bad driver," he said, when their feet came up.

"I haven't had as much practice as you." She nudged his new shoes with her scuffed sneakers, saying, "Those are good-looking shoes you've got there. And long feet. Big, bright, beautiful shoes on the bed."

Clown words! Artie laughed and wiggled his toes. He looked on the screen in his head, but the shadow boy was not there.